THE ROAD THAT LED TO LOVE

Theastarr Valerie

ISBN: 978-1-7338293-8-0

Edited By: Theastarr Valerie, Akilah Valerie – Empress Royále Publishing
Email: empressroyalepublishing@gmail.com

Shaniqua L. Howell – Shelev Publishing
Email: Shelevpublishing@outlook.com

Book Cover Credit Info:

Cover Design: Empress Royále Publishing

Cover Photos: "Chic Table" from Chimene Gaspar (Pexels.com)

"Map Postcard" from xxolgaxx (Pixabay.com)

Empress Royále Publishing

"Everything tells a story; let us help you tell your story to the world."

Email: empressroyalepublishing@gmail.com

Dedication

This book is dedicated to all the women who've felt pressured to get married at a certain age; those who've heard the words, **"when are you getting married?"** on countless occasions over the years. And while you've tried to dodge the question, deep down you ask God, "What about me?" "When will it be my time?" The tears you've cried over the years are now non-existent. Now you no longer think about marriage.

There is nothing new under the sun. Many times we've tried to do things "our way" in the waiting process. Internally screaming, "GOD YOU'RE TAKING TOO LONG…" "How many more jokers do I have to entertain?" All those questions and more are summed up in these words… THE. WAIT. IS. WORTH. IT.

Acknowledgements

To the **Author of all authors, God**: Words cannot begin to express my gratitude to You. You are truly the definition of love. Thank You for giving me the gift of expression through words. Thank You Holy Spirit for letting me know when the choices I make isn't Your *best* for me. Thank You for protecting me from my idea of a "husband" and showing me that my husband **is** a true Man of God. I pray that everything I write would point persons to Your Son, Jesus Christ.

My Papito: My support system since before I could even speak. You continuously encourage me to push through and never allow anything to keep me down. Thank you for demonstrating what it means for a man to love a woman as Christ loves the church. I've cried to you countless times over the decades and you always have a positive response. These words not only allow me to look at things from another perspective, but it also makes me smile. I learned how to research from you, which is integral in writing. Thank you for being a true gentleman and letting me know that I deserve the *best*.

My Madre: Not only did you give birth to me, but you're the reason I'm a writer today. Thank you for exercising the spirit of discernment. For letting me know when "he isn't the one". Thank you for your unadulterated guidance. I appreciate that you're always REAL, telling it like it is. No sugar coating. I couldn't have asked for a better mother. Thank you for reading to me and studying while I was in your womb. To this day you still read and always push yourself to learn more.

I love you Papito and Madre…

Aleah (the Bam to my Bim, my twin, aka Princess): My day one chica. Best little sister anyone could ever ask for. Thanks for always telling me, "you could do this… you got this…" So many times I've come to you for advice and you always know what to say. Thanks for always pushing me to greatness; never allowing me to wallow in self-doubt. Thanks for being an inspiration to me.

Akilah (my Kiki, Da LADii): My reader; number one critic. Best baby sister ever. Thanks for showing interest in what I write. Thanks for reading my books and giving honest feedback and criticism. You taught me not "to describe the color blue". *Hehe.* The amount of hours, days, years you've spent responding to my questions, sharing your expertise on topics I had no clue on, listening to idea after idea, staying up late nights just so I can make sense out of an outline, telling me what works from what doesn't… I am eternally grateful for the integral role you played in this book. I look forward to seeing your published books one day.

Clauressa Weekes (my Reese's): My big sister, my sounding board. I remember how excited you were when I shared the idea for this story. You've encouraged me to become a better writer, always pushing me to think outside of the box. Thanks for continuously asking me about my book publication date. It's **FINALLY** here.

Giselle Johnson: Thank you for not giving up on me. You are a true confidant and I am grateful to have you as my big sister and prayer partner. You taught me how to exercise the spirit of discernment and that is a lesson I would never forget. Thank you for your perpetual excitement in the seemingly "little" things happening in my life. Truly *Bows and Pops* (insider).

Monique Thomas: As I type this, I can hear the excitement in your voice, "Theastarr STARR…" (Added emphasis on purpose) Hehe. Not only are you my big sister, but a true inspiration to me. I appreciate the countless hours you spent helping me during my writing process.

Shaniqua L. Howell: Where do I even start? Thank you for paving the way for Christian authors who are REAL. No cookie cutter, cutesy books. You tell it RAW and get straight to the point. From the very first book I read from you, you've inspired me. I would read your book and hold my breath wondering if you were going to *go there*. And YOU DID!! Time after time. I remember when I first shared with you that I had a book in the works, the sheer joy that emanated from you. I appreciate the countless hours you've spent answering my many questions. You were never "too busy" to read, respond, or critique. I am forever grateful for the part you played in my journey as an author. Keep on writing those books. I'll see you on the bestsellers list.

My second and third grade teacher **Ms. P. Migdol**: My first teacher in the United States of America. I remember my first spelling test in your class where I was the only student who spelled the word *Albuquerque*, although I never heard it before. You were always smiling and never treated me like a foreigner/"the new student". Thank you.

My fourth grade teacher **Ms. D. Marrone**: To the woman who introduced me to writing books. As a 9 year old, I never thought that a lesson in your class would ignite a spark in me to write many other books. The first book I ever wrote was in your class. Thank you miss.

My eleventh grade teacher **Ms. Chang**: The first person I remember telling me that I write "too much". Not in a way to discourage me, but to let me know that I don't need to be *wordy* to get my thoughts across. It was a back and forth trying to trim down my essays and papers to fit your requirements. Thankfully, you accepted that I write plenty and didn't penalize me for going overboard. Look miss, all the writing has paid off.

My twelfth grade teacher **Ms. Moretti**: My AP English to College English teacher. Thanks for introducing me to books I wouldn't have desired to read on my own; books that increased my vocabulary. You were always happy to read and grade my work. I was a bookworm in your class and proud of it.

Nancy Prentice: Thank you for inspiring me to publish my book. You answered my many English and writing related questions; always excited to hear about my passion for writing. I'm grateful for having had the opportunity to work with you.

Gena Mohammed: The BEST LIBRARIAN EVER!! You pushed me to go that extra mile in my writing. Thank you for the opportunities that you gave me to write. Your passion for reading has inspired me. You made me believe that a dream I had for over 19 years could come to pass. I want to thank you from the bottom of my heart.

Extra special shout out to my dog (yes), **Milano P. Marciano**: The most loving and DRAMATIC dog EVER. Thank you for sitting with me while I wrote many of the chapters for this book. It's the simplest things. Love you Popo…

Foreword

I have been blessed with the opportunity of having the first chance at reading and doing the foreword for "The Road That Led To Love". This has truly been a humbling experience for me. I have known Theastarr for the past eight years and I must say that she is truly a 'Starr'.

She has woven a beautiful story of love, mystery and fiction, while making sure that God is the centre of it all. While reading, you will find yourself laughing, crying, angry, shocked in totality, and jumping with joy as she takes the reader on a sea of emotions. Leaving one anticipating what is coming next.

I highly encourage the reader to internalize the different messages in this book, as there are many to digest. From learning the importance of waiting on God, to making sure the spirit of discernment is active in one's life. There is definitely something in this book for every believer. I pray this book ministers to you as it did to me.

Congratulations on your first published book Starr, this is only the beginning. You are indeed a phenomenal woman and I am excited to see all that God will do with your writing career.

One down, many to go!

Shaniqua Howell,

Author: #Diary of a Girl

The Waiting Room

Confessions of Scarred Souls

A Girl and Her God

Dear Future Husband

Prologue

I never met him, but I'm completely in love with him. When I was 8 years old I saw him for the first time on TV. I watched every show and movie he acted in and swooned. He is THE definition of *FINATION*. I had to make up a word to describe him. Yes, I know wishful thinking. As if I would EVER meet him. As if he would EVER like me…

"Earth to Tahira," Kaiora sings.

"We are supposed to be studying," Tahira replies.

Kaiora Marzocco had been Tahira's firecracker best friend for the past two years. Her mouth was known to get her in trouble at times; she held nothing back.

"I know that, but you zoned out. Daydreaming about that boy again?" she jeers.

"Who?" Tahira asks.

"The one you've liked since you were 8 years old."

"No. I was pondering on our exam tomorrow."

"Good. You need to learn now that it will **never** happen. Our life isn't a movie. Boys like that don't court or marry regular girls like us," Kaiora scolded, while popping a gum in her mouth.

Tahira stands up and declares, "I am **not** a regular girl. I am the daughter of a King."

"So am I, but the Bible speaks about idolatry."

"I haven't idolized anyone."

"Either way, let's stick with reality," Kaiora states nonchalantly.

"Besides, he isn't a believer."

Tahira frowns. "He does believe in Jesus."

"Believing in Jesus and serving HIM are two different things."

"Can we stop with the sermons? I know God's word," Tahira conveys, becoming agitated.

Pointing to the textbooks Kaiora ends the conversation. "Back to our studies."

Tahira begins to twiddle her fingers, zoning Kaiora out as she thinks.

Why is it so impossible for me to marry Tavario Mikos? He could become a Christian, like really serving Jesus. SIGH!! Who am I kidding? As Kaiora said, this isn't the movies...

1

"Tahira, are you packed for your 21st birthday trip next week?" Kaiora inquires walking out of her bathroom brushing her hair.

"Yeah girl. *Martin Villagio*, Grand Sierra Isla here we come," Tahira cheers excitedly.

"Maybe we can find you a boyfriend there," she winks.

"I'm good Kaiora, that's not on my agenda. I have my studies. Ministry. Joining *#EnfuegoMissions* in a few months."

"I can't believe you want to be a Missionary. Such a waste of life. You could be the CEO in a big company with your skills and abilities," the words pour out of her mouth like venom.

"Given by God. Missions isn't a *waste of life*. We are all called to fulfill the Great Commission," Tahira corrects.

Kaiora yawns. "Sounds boring. How much do you even get paid as a Missionary?"

"God takes care of those HE has called."

"Girl, you sound pathetic," Kaiora leers. "This is the real world. No one graduates from University to become a Missionary. We're in 2016."

"Wow, thanks for your support bestie."

"I'm being real."

"I am being led," Tahira replies.

"Whatever. Back to your birthday trip. Oops, I forgot to book the tickets."

"Kaiora, what if they're sold out?"

"I got this, trust me." Kaiora grabs her cell from the dresser. "I'm going online now to search for last minute cheap tickets."

"Alright message me later when you get the information. I'm going to my parents' house," Tahira says heading out the door.

> **Incoming News Alert: Tavario Mikos spotted last night with his girlfriend of two years at the premiere of...**

Why did I opt to have these alerts sent to my phone? It's been 13 years since I've liked him, maybe I should forget Tavario and focus on reality. He will never choose me. We don't even move in the same circle...

The drive to her childhood home was short. Only 20 minutes from her best friend's house.

"Hi mom, what was so urgent that you insisted I come over right away?" Tahira calls out to her mother in the kitchen.

"I found your husband," her mother announces when Tahira sits down on a kitchen stool.

Tahira's eyes pop open. "Excuse me? YOU found my husband? I

thought *he* was supposed to find me."

"Don't get sass with me," Tahiti reprimands her daughter. "You know what I mean. I know of someone who would be a perfect fit for you."

"Why do I even indulge you? I told you I'm **not** interested in relationships right now. After graduation I am joining *#EnfuegoMissions*. You've heard me say this for years, mom."

"Missions can wait," Tahiti dismisses. "Or he can go with you."

"It doesn't work that way mother. My husband *is* a Missionary."

"Things change sweetie. Some people learn their purpose later on in life."

"I'm not promising anything, who is it?" Tahira probes.

"Cadell Manantes."

"NO!! No. No. No. Something about him screams **trouble**."

"You need to stop being judgmental Tahira. You're getting older. Do you want to become like those women in church who's never been married?" her mother appeals.

"Don't speak about them like that. Everyone's walk is different. I'm only 21. Still have time. I'm not being judgmental, but discerning. From the moment he started attending our church—"

"What's wrong with him?" Tahiti interrupts. "He is the Young Men's Ministry Director and he plays the PIANO; your favorite instrument. Not to mention how he worships God and speaks in tongues," she continues listing Cadell's attributes.

"Really? That's your defense? He appears moral on *paper*? Have you actually heard his tongues? Or just viewed him from the pews? I know you've heard of the men and women who have titles and seemingly perfect images and how they have fallen short. Pretending." Tahira sighs annoyingly.

"Not this young man. Look at his family. His father is a Prophet and his mother an Evangelist. It doesn't get better than that in godly heritage."

"With all due respect mother, you've taught me how to hear God for myself. Don't allow yourself to be used to mess up the path God has for me. Something is off with him, I'm telling you."

"What if you're wrong?"

"Then let God tell me that."

"Give him a chance honey. Please for me?" her mother beseeches.

"I'll think about it."

Maybe mom is right. I shouldn't judge him. And rightfully so the next step after graduation is marriage…

2

On Wednesday night, a few days after they'd returned from celebrating Tahira's 21st birthday, Kaiora went over to Tahira's house for a last minute pre-date prep talk.

"You're going on a date with the **hottest** man in church." Kaiora screams as Tahira got ready for her date.

"I don't think he's all that. He's no Tavario Mikos."

"Will you **stop** with that man already? You're **never** going to be with him. Let's think about men in our own circle," Kaiora snaps.

Tahira turns to face her bestie. "How do I look?"

"Like a nun."

Tahira examines herself in the mirror. "Good. I don't want him to get any ideas. I don't like him."

"That's what you're saying now. I bet soon you'll be engaged."

"Girl its one date. Let's not jump to engagements." Tahira pauses before asking her next question. "Is it just me or do you think something is off with Cadell?"

"It's just you." Kaiora points at Tahira in the mirror. "You've never had a boyfriend so you don't know how relationships work."

"As opposed to your plethora of boyfriends over the years. I guess that makes you an expert?"

"OF COURSE."

Tahira gives Kaiora a side eye. "Why aren't you engaged? Or married?"

"When I'm ready, I haven't found the right one yet."

"Kaiora, you're not supposed to find any man. *He who findeth a wife, findeth a good thing*—"

"There you go preaching again. Are you sure you're not called to be a Pastor? You're always preaching."

"This isn't funny. I'm stating what the Word of God says. When we were younger you were the preacher. Now you don't behave like a young lady who grew up in church at all."

"I grew out of that lifestyle," Kaiora scoffs. "You sound like a judgmental **old** Christian who needs to loosen up."

"I'm your best friend. If I can't speak the truth in love then what's the point?"

"Let's drop the topic. I hear Cadell's horn. Do you have your vex money?"

"You know it," Tahira responds, placing a wallet in her purse.

"Tahira, you look beautiful," Cadell compliments when she opens the door.

"Thanks."

"You ready to go?"

"Sure," Tahira retorts, walking towards his car.

"Why so frank? Don't you want to go out with me? I don't bite," he replies, trying to keep up with her pace.

"Um."

Cadell pauses from opening the car door. "Did I do something wrong?"

"No," Tahira shrugs.

"Are you going to be speaking monosyllabic the entire date?"

"Maybe," she responds nonchalantly.

"I brought this for you."

Tahira takes the object. "How'd you know I love keychains?"

"I've liked you for a while and I pay attention," he reveals. "I heard you mention that you love other cultures and can't wait to travel to collect keychains from all over the world. My folks just returned from *Covingo District* in *Night Harbor*, Mt. Thafivin and gave me this. I decided to give it to you. You can start your collection."

"Oh wow, thanks. I don't know what to say."

"10 words; I am making progress," Cadell laughs.

Tahira giggles.

Maybe he isn't so bad after all.

"I have one stop to make," Cadell says exiting the car 30 minutes later.

"No problem." Tahira looks up and sees **Lucky Helix Casino** written on the building.

Why is he going in there? Calm down, don't judge.

After a tiresome drive to their location Cadell spreads a blanket at a quaint spot in the park. "I hope you don't mind your first date being a picnic. I love the outdoors."

"It's fine. Sweet. Different from the typical first date," Tahira asserts.

"Here try this," he places a piece of *Sun Braised Brisket* into her mouth.

"I can feed myself thanks," she grimaces.

"I wasn't trying to be inappropriate." Cadell puts the meat back into the container.

Tahira nervously twiddles with her fingers. "It's not you. I don't know what to expect from a date."

"Relax. As I said, I don't bite."

What happens on a first date? I guess every situation is different. There isn't a manual on first date protocol. Is there?

Snapping out of her thoughts, Tahira takes a sip of her drink. "Tell me about yourself."

"I'm 25 years old as you know. I graduated with my Masters in Finance. I'm called into *Missions,* but still shaky about the decision," Cadell discloses nervously.

A light goes off in her head. "Missions?"

It can't be.

Cadell chuckles, "Sounds like an oxymoron huh? A finance man entering into the lowest paying career on the planet."

"It sounds wonderful. After I graduate I want to go into the Missions field full time. Have you heard of *#EnfuegoMissions?*"

"Can't say that I have. I hope you can tell me about it someday. I've never met a woman with similar interest when it comes to *Missions*. Usually they want to marry and have a *perfect life*. Not get down in the trenches." Cadell stares at her, impressed at her excitement.

"This is crazy."

"What is?"

"N-nothing. I'm shocked that's all."

Cadell looks at his watch. "It's getting late Tahira; I should take you back to your house."

Tahira rummages through her purse for her keys. "Thanks for a great first date Cadell."

"I would love to take you on a second. Saturday at 4pm. There's a nature exhibit in the museum gardens I'd like you to see."

She nods in acceptance. "Ok, sounds good."

"Excellent. See you then."

3

When she arrives in her room, Tahira immediately dials her best friend.

Kaiora picks up on the first ring.

"Girlllllllll Cadell wants to be a **Missionary**," Tahira shrieks into the receiver. "I did everything from screaming in excitement. That was the BEST first date."

"See, I told you. You were judging him for no reason. He may be your husband."

At the mention of the word *husband* Tahira pauses, "It's possible. I have to pray about it."

"What for?

Christian ☑

Good looking ☑

Into Missions ☑

Everything you want ☑ " Kaiora lists.

"He may not be God's will for my life."

"I don't mean to roll my eyes girl, but God gave us Free Will for a reason.

Who we marry is **our** choice," Kaiora mumbles.

"It is, but being in God's perfect will is important to me. A spouse could make or break purpose," Tahira proclaims.

"You need to stop."

"Speaking the truth?"

"Not going to argue with you. However, send me a picture of what you're going to wear for your next date. No more NUN outfits."

"Kaiora, the date's 3 days away."

"I'm waiting."

The clock was seconds away from midnight and Tahira knelt down by her bedside to pray, eager to speak with her Heavenly Father.

Dear Father God, I come to You in the name of Jesus asking for Your guidance. Is Cadell Your perfect will for my life?

The answer came to her immediately. **NO.**

"Good morning, my child," Ramiro says the next morning, handing his daughter a piping hot cup of *Cobalt Tea*.

"Thanks dad," Tahira responds, accepting the tea. "Can we talk?"

"Sure sweetie. Have a seat."

"It's about a man."

"Cadell?"

"Yes, what do you think of him?" she exhales waiting for her father's reply.

"Do you want my honest opinion or what you want to hear?"

"I'm afraid at either answer."

Ramiro takes a moment to choose his words wisely. "I don't like that boy. His entire family isn't what they portray to be. Be careful. I know it is your decision and I pray that you make the best one. Ask God to order your steps."

"That's just it. Last night I prayed and the answer I got was **NO**," Tahira laments.

"Well my child, what else do you need to hear?"

"I think it was me being scared because it was my first date."

"We've taught you the ways of the Lord and you've been doing well thus far. I won't tell you what to do. I love you and want the best for you. If I could pick a man to be your husband, it would not be Cadell. Don't make any hasty decisions. I will go to jail for murder if any man hurts my baby."

"That's not Christ-like."

"Be warned," Ramiro cautions.

Hours later Tahira found herself in the middle of the Manantes' living room.

"I'd like you to officially meet my parents," Cadell announces.

"Prophet Quintos and Evangelist Cyra it's nice to be welcomed in your home," Tahira greets apprehensively.

"Call us Mr. and Mrs. Manantes. No official titles necessary. As our son's friend, we're excited to have you," Cyra beams.

"Shall we sit down to eat?" Quintos signals.

Cadell pulls out a chair for Tahira.

"Thanks," she smiles.

"Let's dig in," Cadell's father declares.

"Um," Tahira looks across at the family already devouring their meal, "aren't we going to pray?"

"We don't pray for our food," Mr. Manantes murmurs in between bites. "Our morning devotions cover all prayers so we're prayed up for the entire day."

Tahira stares at the older gentleman, "You all only pray once a day? Strange."

"Nothing strange dear; where we come from we were taught the importance of *one prayer covers all*. We've been doing that since we first became converts in Mt. Thafivin," Cyra enlightens.

Tahira glances at the woman, hoping that her true thoughts weren't revealed on her face. "I never heard of it before, but I'm still learning about different cultures. Whatever works for you all is cool with me. Thanks for sharing a part of your culture with me Mrs. Manantes."

"Shall we continue the meal?" Mrs. Manantes asks, shutting down any further conversation on the topic.

Tahira picks up her fork. "Yes, everything looks delicious."

4

Tahira called her best friend the following morning to update her on the awkward dinner experience at the Manantes'.

"They only pray once a day. Not even before they eat. Apparently where they come from the morning devotional prayer covers all prayers for the day."

Kaiora laughs. "Well Tahira you said you want to be a Missionary."

"I AM a Missionary."

"Okay Ms. Missionary. Look at this as your first lesson. Not all cultures are the same. And even though they only pray once a day, it doesn't mean they aren't believers. Don't go into Missions looking at other cultures through the lens of ours."

After a moment's reflection, Tahira continues. "I understand, but prayer… That's something that Jesus our greatest example did more than once a day. As HIS followers we are supposed to emulate HIM."

"HE was crucified. Are we all supposed to die too?" Kaiora teases.

"Galatians 5:24 '*And they that are Christ's have crucified the flesh with the affections and lusts.*'"

"Moving on."

"Why do you always try to shut me down when I speak about Jesus or God's Word? I expect that from an unsaved person, but not from one who professes Christ."

"Because you act like we live in Biblical times where everything is about temple, sermons and commandments. We live in the 21st Century. We can be Christians, but not old fashioned," Kaiora yawns loudly.

"Old fashioned? God's Word is as relevant today as when it was written."

"I just mean, we've grown up in Church and we're 21 now. Let's live a little. God would understand. HE did put us on this Earth."

"Yes, we're in it, but not *of* it," Tahira stresses.

Kaiora begins to chuckle. "I could clap all day at your sermons. You'll make a powerful minister someday, but right now **enjoy life**. You're too young to be so serious about Christianity."

"Well I never... What nonsense are you speaking about?"

"Personally, I'm over the whole Christianity thing. I go to church because it is the right thing to do. I believe in God, Jesus Christ and the Holy Spirit, but as far as I am concerned Christianity is for old people."

"I'm sorry you feel that way Kaiora," Tahira admits. "I pray that you have an encounter with God for yourself so that HE becomes real to you and not just someone you read/heard about. Christianity is a *relationship* not a religion. Until you get that, there's nothing I can do or say to convince you. And I won't try to. I will pray."

5

Cadell pulls up into Tahira's driveway. "We're here. Who are you looking at on your phone?"

"No one, I'm checking on the latest trends," Tahira responds without fully acknowledging him.

"Trends make you blush?"

"I'm blushing? Really? Hadn't noticed."

"Look at me," Cadell demands sullenly. "Am I crazy or am I competing with a fantasy?"

"I don't understand," she replies flatly.

"That man you're watching. You think I haven't noticed him as your screensaver?"

"No need to get jealous, he's an actor. I'm never going to see him in real life."

"This is what you're saying to *me*. But, it seems as though you're in a one-sided emotional relationship with this man." His voice increases, "Is this what you're going to do when we're married?"

"Why are you yelling?" She turns her gaze from him. "Besides, who's talking about marriage?"

"Look at me when I'm talking to you. You're being disrespectful to me. How would you feel if I had a picture of another woman on my phone?"

Tahira rolls her eyes. "He's an ACTOR Cadell. Jeez. What is the big deal?"

"I'm a man and I am telling you I don't like it."

"We're not in a relationship. Why are you behaving this way?"

"You think I'm playing games with you? We've been hanging out for weeks," Cadell bellows.

"Yes, but you haven't officially asked me to be your girlfriend. Unless you're clear about your intentions, I'm a free agent. You can't be making demands of me if we're just friends."

"I don't spend all this time with friends. You're more than a friend to me."

"That doesn't equate to anything. Until you ask—"

"Tahira, would you be my girlfriend?" Cadell interjects.

"Was that so hard? Now we're official and I will delete the picture of Tavario," she sneers internally.

"Kaiora, you should've seen how upset he got when I was looking at Tavario's picture," Tahira laughs when she reaches inside her house.

"I told you it'd work. We're too old for guessing games. He had to make his intentions known."

"I didn't think it was a big deal until you explained how relationships work."

"I am the best."

"When do you think you'd settle down though? Being a player isn't a good sign as a Christian woman."

"PLEASE DO NOT START," Kaiora yells heatedly. "I helped you with Cadell and his commitment phobia. Don't try to give me lectures on morality."

"All I'm saying is it's time to settle down."

"Why is it okay for a man to *test the waters* before marriage and we females can't?"

"No one should be testing any waters. You're supposed to seek the Lord," Tahira corrects.

"Honestly, I don't care. It's my life and I am going to do whatever I want. I'm not hurting anyone. I'm not having sex with any of the men I date," Kaiora responds casually.

"You're hurting yourself. The time you're wasting dating a bunch of men you could be waiting on the **one** for you."

"I'm not interested in your fairytale version of life. 'The One'? Oh please. That's hogwash."

"I want the best for you Kaiora."

"I appreciate it, but I'm good. I want to make all the mistakes of life while I still have my youth."

6

"How was school today honey?" Tahiti asks Tahira during lunch the next day.

"School was great. We have finals in a few weeks and then I'm off to join *#EnfuegoMissions*."

"Are you sure you don't want to get a full-time job first? Maybe go on a Missions trip during vacation?"

"Mom, I'm not lacking in the finance department. I've saved up enough money to live comfortably for at least a year. Plus, I still get my regular weekly paychecks from my part-time job."

"That's all well and good, but I don't believe you should throw your life away," her mother replies.

Tahira pauses from stirring the pot. "Are you and Kaiora twins? Why do you refer to Missions as a waste? Do you know that there are over 3 billion persons who haven't even heard the name of Jesus?"

"I know the stats, but you could be a giver to someone else going onto the field. So much potential for you to work in a big firm."

"Thank you for your concern," Tahira nods. "However, my aim in life is to please God, not man."

"Okay, once as you know what you're doing," Tahiti rescinds.

"Back to the original reason I came over. I need your advice."

"About?" Tahiti pulls up a chair and motions for her daughter to sit.

"You've been married to daddy for 25 years, together for even longer. Has he ever been jealous of another man because of you?"

Tahiti tilts her head back in a hearty laugh. "When your father and I started courting I had a best friend who I hung out with all the time. We grew up together and your father insisted that my best friend liked me and he didn't like us hanging out together. He felt *disrespected*."

"What's with men and that word? So what did you do?"

"I had a conversation with my friend, explaining what your father told me and he admitted that he did like me. I was in shock because I never viewed him in that manner. Then he told me we could no longer be friends. He was waiting for the right time to tell me that he had feelings for me and when your father came along he knew that his opportunity was gone."

Tahira claps. "Go mom. Two guys fighting over you."

"No one fought honey. We had a grown up conversation and all made the right choice for ourselves."

"Have you seen or heard from him since?"

"The last time I saw him was at our High School Reunion 10 years ago. He was happily married with 5 children," Tahiti reminisces.

"I guess you're both with the right spouse."

"What is your predicament though? Who's jealous of whom?"

"Cadell is jealous of Tavario."

"I thought you were over that actor?"

"Over him? We never dated."

"Your crush. I know you've liked him since you were a little girl. His picture is still on your wall at your house. I didn't say anything because I thought eventually you'd have grown out of it. But, this is ridiculous."

"Kaiora told me that if Cadell saw Tavario's picture as my screensaver, he would get jealous, man up and ask me to be his girlfriend."

"Don't play games Tahira. You're a woman. Those stunts are for teens."

"Why would he be jealous of a man who I don't even know mom? Who I've never seen in real life?"

"A person only puts pictures as their screensaver if they like it. You had a picture of another **man** on your screen. A young, good looking man at that. That's something that Cadell would take note of."

"It's deleted anyway," Tahira laughs, "I'm glad that he finally asked me to be his girlfriend instead of dancing around the topic."

"And while you're at it, take Tavario's picture off your wall. You need to get yourself emotionally free to marry Cadell," Tahiti implores.

7

Kaiora joined Tahira at her house an hour later.

"Ready?" Kaiora asks holding the matchbox.

"Ready. Wait, wait. Can't we just throw the picture away?" Tahira grips the photo.

"It's symbolic. By burning the picture you are declaring that you're burning away desires and chances of being with Tavario."

"But what if I have a chance?"

Kaiora pulls the photo from Tahira's hands. "We're doing this. It's for your own good."

"It's not that easy," Tahira laments. "He's had my heart since I was a little girl."

"The entire country knows that. But in our reality he isn't real. He doesn't know you exist. Let him go."

"I don't want to."

"Are you pouting? Girl you'd better get over it. You're going to marry Cadell," Kaiora admonishes.

"He hasn't even proposed to me."

Kaiora opens the matchbox. "Trust me, he will."

"How do you know?"

"That man is very determined to make you his wife. I see it, feel it and know it. You can't deny that he loves you."

"I don't think I am ready for marriage," Tahira discloses.

"You're definitely ready."

"How could I marry Cadell if I love Tavario?"

"SNAP OUT OF IT," Kaiora shouts. "Tavario is in a relationship. Why are you lusting after him and coveting another woman's boyfriend?"

"Don't say that. I'm not lusting or coveting."

"Oh, so now you don't want to hear the Word of God?"

"You're twisting it."

"Tahira, you're in a relationship with Cadell; a real man who loves you. Though you may think you love Tavario, it won't happen. Better to accept that now than pine over him for the rest of your life *hoping* that you'll be together."

"What's wrong with hoping?" Tahira challenges.

"At some point there are things we all have to let go. We don't always get what we want in life and we must accept it."

"Such negative vibes. Why can't I hope for the impossible?"

"You can, but not this. Men like that don't marry women like us. Are you ready to burn his picture?" Kaiora says holding both picture and match.

"Okay, you're right. Let's do it."

As the flame engulfs the photo, a tear falls from Tahira's eye.

8

On Monday morning Tahira parked her car in front of her workplace. As she walked towards the elevator a man bumps into her.

"Watch where you're going!" she snaps.

"I'm sorry, today is my first day and I'm in a hurry," the man apologizes. "I want to make a good impression. Can you tell me where the Senior VP's office is?" he asks.

"I'm on my way there now. My name is Tahira, what's yours?"

"Vassos."

"Where are you from Vassos?" Tahira clicks the elevator button for floor **18**.

"Chania, Greece."

"You're a foreigner?" she shrieks.

"I am. Is that a bad thing?"

"I've never met someone who isn't a citizen of Starr Islands. What is Greece like? I'm a Missionary and can't wait to travel the world."

Vassos smiles at Tahira. "Let's have dinner and I'll tell you about my country. I can show you pictures as well. Maybe one day I can take you there."

"That would be awesome," Tahira giggles, "A Greek man. One can only read about it in books."

They exit the elevator. Tahira walks with him to the office.

"This is my first time in Starr Islands," Vassos shares.

Tahira wanted to know all about the foreigner. "How'd you end up in our lovely country?"

"Work Abroad Internship."

"I am so excited. I can show you the ropes. What to do, where to eat, the works."

"Is everyone in Starr Islands this friendly?"

"Hehe. Maybe," Tahira grins.

"Good night, how many in your party?"

"Three. The third person is on his way," Tahira informs the waitress at the entrance of the restaurant that night.

"Right this way ladies," the waitress escorts them to their table.

"Thank you," Tahira and Kaiora say in unison when handed their menus.

"I will be back shortly to take your orders," the waitress announces.

Kaiora knocks on the table. "Who is it that you wanted me to meet tonight?"

"Hold on, there he is." Tahira motions for Vassos to join them.

"*Oraía na synantíso ómorfi kyría,*" Vassos greets when he arrives at the table.

"What's he saying?" Kaiora looks at Tahira puzzled.

"I said, *nice to meet you beautiful lady,*" he translates.

"Vassos, this is Kaiora my best friend. Kaiora this is Vassos, he's Greek."

Kaiora was not impressed by his charm. "Does that line work in Greece?"

Noting the apprehension in Kaiora's countenance, Vassos adds, "It's not a line. I am being polite and truthful."

"Hey you two," Tahira waves, "I'm still here. Can I join in the convo?"

"Jealous much?" Kaiora chuckles, finally loosening up. "I'm getting to know your new friend."

"No jealousy," Tahira recants. "Let's **all** enjoy dinner."

"Thanks for inviting me out tonight Tahira."

"You're welcome. I promised Vassos I'd show him around town. He's a new intern."

Kaiora rolls her eyes. "I gathered that from the convo."

"I'm glad you came though. It would've been awkward going out with a man who isn't my boyfriend."

"You're planning on having more outings with Vassos?"

"A little," she shrugs, "until he learns how to get around Fortazonio."

"Be careful. It's not your duty to be Vassos' tour guide. Now's not the time to be getting all friendly with men," Kaiora warns.

"I'm not doing anything," Tahira retorts defensively.

"A picture of another man is one thing, actually hanging out with him? You're asking for trouble."

9

"Congratulations on your graduation honey. We're proud of you," Tahiti squeals.

"Awwwww. Thanks mom and dad. You all have been my support team from day one. This degree is dedicated to you. I love you," Tahira embraces her parents.

"It was sweet of you to take a day off from work to support our daughter on her graduation day, Cadell."

"I wouldn't have it any other way Mrs. Zagori. She is my girlfriend. One day she'll be my wife. I love her."

"Such a lovely young man," Tahiti affirms.

"Mr. Zagori do I have your permission to take your daughter on a graduation lunch date?"

Ramiro looks sternly at Cadell, "This was supposed to be family time."

Tahiti stares at her husband. "Leave the young people alone. You all go ahead."

Tahira and Cadell walk away holding hands.

"Why do you undermine my authority? I told you I do not like him. If he *ever* asks me for permission to marry my daughter the answer is **no**."

"UNDERMINE YOUR AUTHORITY?" Tahiti scoffs. "This isn't the 1950s Ramiro. Stop being old fashioned. She's 21."

"I don't even know who you are anymore."

"I am the woman you married."

"The woman I married had respect for me. You don't care about what I have to say. If anything happens to my daughter I WILL hurt that young man."

"Do you hear yourself, Mr. *Elder*?"

Not being offended by his wife's jibe, Ramiro continues, "She's my only child. It is my duty as her father and the head of this family to protect her. To give her away to the man who is to be her husband. Cadell is NOT her husband."

"You're not a member of the Trinity, how would you know that?"

"She's not marrying him. This conversation is over," Ramiro says trying to prevent a full scale dispute.

When they arrived at the lunch venue, Tahira's eyes widen. "Why are we here?"

"It's where I work."

"You work in the casino?"

"Is that a problem?" Cadell snaps.

"We've been courting—"

"Dating," he corrects. "I don't use ancient terms."

Tahira rolls her eyes. "We've been *dating* for 5 months and I never knew you worked at a casino. I thought you worked at **TDFC**?"

"I do. I also work at the casino; paying off debts," Cadell states opening the door.

"What debts? You got a scholarship to University."

"Personal debts."

Tahira pauses midway through the door and looks at her boyfriend. "Were you planning on telling me about these debts? Isn't this something I should know if we are to marry one day?"

"Well you're finding out today. I am a very private man."

"Why are you speaking to me like that? Since when am I not allowed to ask you questions? I'm your girlfriend."

"Yes, but NOT MY WIFE," Cadell barks.

"Don't raise your voice at me. Sorry for caring. Sorry for asking."

"No need to apologize baby. I am sorry." Cadell touches her arm, "I should've told you. Just didn't want to scare you away."

"Why would that scare me away?"

"I don't know, in the past when a woman found out the real me, she ran away. Will you run away, if I'm one hundred percent honest with you?"

Tahira places her arms around his neck. "I won't. Honesty is healthy for a relationship."

10

"Cadell, are you on duty today?" a woman asks moments later.

"No. Today is my pretty lady's graduation day and I want her to experience **Lucky Helix Casino's** finest lunch with all the trimmings."

"It's about time we get to meet her," the woman answers.

"He talks about me?" Tahira joins in.

The woman nods, "All the time. Always showing off your picture to the staff."

Tahira looks at Cadell with a playful grin on her face.

"My love, I'll be back. I want to ask the chef to add a special item for your lunch."

"I'll be waiting." Tahira blushes as Cadell trots away. Swinging back on the bar stool she summons the woman behind the bar serving drinks to customers. "What's your name?"

The woman points to her tag, "The name's Siren. Can I get you a drink?"

"No thanks, I don't drink. I wanted to ask you about Cadell."

Siren waves her finger at Tahira, "Baby girl, I don't get involved in the business of my coworkers."

"Woman to woman, what do you think about him?" Tahira asks,

ignoring Siren's disclaimer.

Siren shrugs, "My opinion doesn't matter. Are you happy with him?"

"I am. However, this is the first time I've met any of his 'people' outside of his parents. He doesn't have any friends in church besides me."

"WAIT, Cadell is a CHURCH BOY? HA!! Could've fooled me," Siren jeers.

Tahira looks at Siren in disdain. "Why is that funny?"

"The way he acts around here; getting into brawls, cursing out customers. His nickname is *Sailorman*."

"Really? He curses?"

"I thought I had a dirty mouth, but he's got me beat," Siren whispers.

"I find that hard to believe."

"As I said I don't like to get involved in my coworkers' business. But, woman to woman I'd advise you to stay away from him. He has a $4.4 million debt in this casino. That's why he has to work here. He works for no pay. Your face expression tells me this is news to you."

"He did tell me he has personal debts, b-but $4.4 million?"

"Boss man doesn't take well to people who try to scam him. Cadell is lucky that boss man likes him. He brings in tons of customers. The ladies love him."

"Has he had relations with any of them? Like you know—" Tahira stops midsentence.

"Oh you mean sex? Not that I know of. I don't know how he does it, but he draws lots of female clientele. Probably has to do with his real job."

"You mean the finance company?"

"Have you ever looked it up? What he does exactly?"

"It's a finance company."

"They do finance alright," Siren gives Tahira a look. "Not the type you expect. Cadell is the owner and CEO of the largest underground match making site for lonely women looking for love. They pay him big money to hook them up with men. The casino is where they usually meet for first dates. So the more clients he has the more his debt decreases. Boss man is very generous."

Tahira takes a moment to process the information. "You're saying my boyfriend is a con artist?"

"As I said I don't like to discuss my coworkers. Here he comes."

"Why are you looking at me like that?" Cadell asks handing Tahira a drink, to which she declines.

"You LIED TO ME!!" she screams.

"Can we talk outside? I don't want to cause a scene."

"Why didn't you tell me you have a debt of $4.4 million? That you basically own a modern day brothel?" Tahira fumes.

"Will you keep your voice down?"

"OUCH! Why'd you pinch me?" she rubs her arm.

"Sorry, reflex," Cadell apologizes.

"You're a con artist. I knew something was wrong with you. I should've gone with my guts. You're a liar. Are you even a Christian?"

"Because I have issues, I'm not a Christian?" Cadell scoffs.

"You have more than issues. Was anything you said the truth? Do you even want to be a Missionary?"

"Tahira, have I ever lied to you? I love you. I do want to be a Missionary. That's what I was shaky about on our first date. Remember I told you that? The only reason I am doing this is to repay the debt I owe the casino. All of this happened before I converted, but I can't abandon my responsibilities. I want to clear my debt before I go away for *Missions*."

"We'll work it out," Tahira sighs.

"You're not going to leave me?"

Tahira shakes her head. "You're right. Everyone has issues. We'll work this out together. That's love."

"One of the many reasons I love you. I knew I chose right, when I chose you." Cadell embraces her.

11

"How does it feel to be a part of the graduating class of 2016? Do you want to go out and celebrate?" Vassos inquires later that afternoon over video chat.

"It feels great," Tahira beams. "Let's go watch *War of Doors*, the new movie with Tavario Mikos."

"I see someone's got a crush," he teases.

"Shhhhh. Don't tell anyone."

"Your secret's safe with me." Vassos motions a zipped lip. "I can't wait until you meet my girlfriend in person. Maybe we can double date when she gets here."

"That might be an issue."

"Why?"

"Cadell isn't into movies."

"What man isn't into a good action film? We can do something else then. Maybe visit another Starr Island. I'm sure she'd love that."

"When is Olympia coming again?" Tahira probes.

"July 4th."

"Vassos, that's two weeks away."

"I know and I'm looking forward to it. Two months with my lady. Are you sure that she could stay by your house?"

"Of course, you're like a brother to me. She's practically my sister-in-law. Greek wedding bells soon."

"You first."

"You think Cadell will propose?"

"He'd be a fool not to."

12

Her graduation day was filled with mixed emotions. The movie surpassed her expectations. Tahira was glad to have a friend who supported her unrequited love for Tavario Mikos. Just then the doorbell rings.

Who could it be at this hour? It's almost midnight.

Tahira opens the door and sees Kaiora standing with her arms folded.

"Can we talk?" Kaiora asks in a monotonous voice.

"Yeah girl. What's up?"

"I think this is the end of the road when it comes to our friendship."

Tahira stares in shock. "What are you talking about?"

"We're not on the same page anymore. I haven't been to church in over three months and my lifestyle isn't conducive for judgmental people," Kaiora states, getting straight to the point.

"I don't judge you Kaiora."

"I feel bad being around you. Like at any moment you'd call me out for something I am doing."

"You know what's right from wrong. What you're experiencing is called conviction."

"This is exactly what I am speaking about. You always do this. I want to live my life free of your sermons."

Tahira places her hand on Kaiora's shoulder. "You're going through a rough patch in your relationship with Jesus. It happens to everyone."

"It doesn't," Kaiora replies, batting Tahira's hand. "You've managed to hold on to your beliefs all these years, but for me... I don't think I ever really believed. Tired of going through the motions."

"Let's pray," Tahira emboldens.

"That's your thing. I'm not into that lifestyle anymore. Goodbye Tahira."

Tahira stands on the porch watching her best friend drive off in her vehicle.

God, what is happening here? First I find out negative traits about my boyfriend and now my best friend ends our friendship?

7 months later

"Good evening Mr. Zagori." Cadell enters the Zagori house, "Can we speak man to man?"

"Look here boy—" Ramiro begins.

"All due respect sir, I want to have a normal conversation for once. I've been dating your daughter for 1 year and you've seemed to hate me from the start. What did I ever do?"

"Tell me Cadell, what is it that you do for a living?"

"I work in Finance."

"That's a vague response. Where exactly do you work?"

"**Trillion Dollar Finance Corp.** I own the business," Cadell announces proudly.

"How come I don't hear much talk about your business?"

"You've never asked. Anything else you want to know before I ask my question?"

"Go ahead with your question."

"You know how much I love your daughter. She is the definition of a Queen. Although it's old fashioned, I know how important it is to her that I do this, so sir—"

"Stop right there," Ramiro gesticulates. "My answer is NO. NO you do NOT HAVE PERMISSION to marry my daughter. I've made that clear from day one. It's nothing against you, but you're not my daughter's husband. Since she was a baby I prayed for the man God will send for her and you are not him."

"Very well. She wanted me to ask and I tried. With or without your permission I am going to propose to your daughter and she will say yes because she loves me. There is nothing you or your archaic views could do about it. STUPID OLD MAN!!" Cadell storms off in a huff.

Tahiti enters the foyer. "My husband what was that all about?"

"That disrespectful boy wanted to ask permission to marry our daughter," Ramiro updates.

The mention of **marry** piques Tahiti's interest. "Oooooooo and what did you say?"

"No!! I've been saying no and I will continue to say no until the right man comes along."

"Why are you trying to deny me happiness?" she cries theatrically.

"You're not happy with me?"

"This isn't about our marriage. I want grandchildren."

Ramiro glares at his wife perplexed. "She's 22. You have enough time to get grandchildren."

"Tomorrow isn't promised to anyone," his wife notes. "What if I don't live to see that day?"

"No talk of death. When God is ready our daughter will get married. But, not to that young man."

13

Tahira and Cadell celebrated the anniversary of their first date that night. It'd been more than ten minutes since she had on the blindfold. The drive to their location took longer than expected.

"Can I take off the blindfold?" Tahira asks agitated with the lengthy drive.

"One minute, I want to make sure everything is perfect," Cadell informs.

"Now?"

"Baby, wait a minute." Cadell turns off the engine. "Okay now." He removes the blindfold then takes her hands.

Tears fall as she observes the scenery in front of her. A walkway lined with candles led to a beautiful lake. As they walked she noted pictures of the two throughout their relationship. He even included the moment she received her degree. At the end of the pathway he had a candlelit dinner set up for them by the lake's edge.

Cadell gets down on one knee. "Tahira from the first time I saw you I knew that there was something special about you. Every day for the year we've been dating has been an adventure. You are my Queen. Would you do me the honor of joining me in a lifelong journey of happiness by becoming—"

Tahira stops his speech, "Did you speak to my father?"

Cadell nods. "I know how important it was that I go to him."

"Well then…"

Cadell holds the ring nervously. "So you'll be my wife?"

"Of course I'll marry you!!" she beams as he places the ring on her finger.

They share a long romantic kiss.

"What did your parents say when you told them you were going to propose?" Tahira inquires when they sit down to eat dinner.

"They are ecstatic. Mom said she can't wait to officially call you *daughter*."

"Being only children is a lot of pressure. My parents will gain a son."

"Your dad doesn't like me much."

"Why do you say that?"

"The way he responded when I went to ask for your hand in marriage."

"Dad's just dad. He doesn't think any man is good enough for his only daughter."

"Do you like the meal?" he points to her food. "I can't wait to cook for you for the rest of our lives."

"You don't mind cooking?"

"I'd love cooking for you. I cook for my parents all the time."

"You're too good to me."

"I am aren't I?"

"Conceited much?" she begins to laugh until he pinches her. "Why'd you pinch me?"

"Watch your words. Don't speak to me like that," Cadell vociferates.

"Does that mean you have to pinch me?"

"If I need to correct you I will."

"Correct me? I am your future wife not child." Tahira rubs her arm.

"That's part of my culture; discipline."

"I'm all for discipline, for our children. But pinching me? That's a little overboard. I'm an adult."

"If you're going to marry me you have to accept my culture."

"Your culture is weird; very different from mine. Try not to pinch so hard," she writhes in pain.

"All you have to do is behave and you'll have no need to get pinched."

"How will I know if I'm misbehaving?"

"You'll learn. Eventually," Cadell dismisses.

What's happening here? I have to do some research on his culture. It's getting weirder by the minute. This pinching seems like abuse to me.

14

Tahira bursts into her parents' house the following day with her big announcement, "MOM. DAD. HE PROPOSED."

Her mom runs into the foyer squealing in excitement. "Let me see the ring. Oh it's beautiful honey. Wedding planning starts now."

"Why do you look indignant dad?"

"I did not give him permission to marry you," Ramiro replies sternly.

"Cadell said he spoke to you."

"He did, but I said no."

"Whatever," Tahira shrugs, "I am happy. He asked. You could've said anything you wanted. The point is he was respectful enough to come to you."

"What has gotten into you? You've never spoken to me like this; never disrespected me."

"I'm getting older and your opinion wouldn't always matter to me," Tahira answers brazenly. "You taught me to make my own choices. I chose Cadell. Why can't you be happy for me? I did all that you required. Went to school. Got a job. Why can't I do what I want now? Get married."

"I have no issue with you getting married. I'd like nothing better. But not to that boy," Ramiro counteracts.

"I know, I know. You don't like him. I think you're finding fault with him because you don't think any man is good enough for your *only daughter* as you keep pointing out."

"That is not it. When I prayed for your husband—" he pauses. "Forget it. A true leader doesn't argue, we pray. I will keep praying for you until that boy is out of your life."

"Don't bother. He is my husband and your prayers have no weight in my life," Tahira responds defiantly.

Tahiti takes Tahira's hand. "Come on Tahira, let's start the wedding plans. I can't wait to tell all the church mothers who have been praying for you two. Everyone will be so excited."

The Manantes' House

"It is finished," Cadell informs his mother at breakfast.

"You proposed?" Cyra grins.

"I did."

"What was her response?"

"Yes, of course. You expected something else?"

"Well the last time you did this you were unsuccessful. I expect you to follow through this time."

"I was careful this time," Cadell explains.

"Good," Cyra smirks. "Our leaders will be pleased. As soon as you are married she is to return with us to our country. She cannot have the influence of outsiders."

15

On Friday night Ramiro joined the elders for their weekly meeting.

"Brother Ramiro what is the matter?" Pastor Nakoa Hizaor asks. "Your countenance is extremely somber."

"Pastor Hizaor, I am losing control over my family. Ever since the Manantes' entered into this congregation and subtly wormed their way into my daughter's life, things have gone awry. My wife has no respect for me and my daughter is engaged to a fool."

"How could you speak about the Prophet and Evangelist like that? Their son is the epitome of leadership. Since he's been here the youth group has grown exponentially. The young people love him."

Ramiro looks around at the room of men. "None of you have daughters and as Tahira's father it is my duty to protect her from the snares of the enemy. I won't allow her to marry that man. No matter what any of you think."

The men remain silent as Ramiro and Pastor Hizaor exchanges words.

"As one of our Senior Elders I respect your feelings and as my brother in Christ I stand by you. We will pray about it; that the truth comes out. When are they to marry?" Pastor Hizaor inquires.

"Their wedding date is set for her 23rd birthday," Ramiro responds.

"We will be praying until then. If nothing happens after the set aside prayer is finished, then you must allow her to marry."

"With all due respect Pastor, she is my daughter. You can't tell me what I must *allow* in my family. But, I do agree with the time of prayer. I will pray that their relationship dissolves."

Meanwhile, in Cadell's house Tahira notices an image she hadn't seen prior.

"Who are those people in the photo?"

"New members from our congregation back home," Cadell replies dryly.

"Why do they look like that? Why are they dressed that way?" Tahira jokes.

"Look like what? That's the dress code for converts back home."

"They look possessed. Like robots or something. Their stares are blank. No one is smiling."

"Let's not judge sweetie."

"Wait… Would I have to dress like that once we get married?"

"As long as we live here in *Jozelle Oasis*, Fortazonio, you can dress like you've been dressing; gorgeous," he compliments.

She blushes.

Tahira exhales. "I know I am old fashioned, but we're in 2017 and it's important that my dress code stays up to date."

Cadell holds up a finger in contention, adding, "If we visit *Covingo District* your attire must be respectful of the culture there."

"I don't mind blending in with the locals. Not a problem. I am learning every day about your culture. I did have a question though."

"Which is?"

"Why isn't there any information on your city? I've looked all over the internet and not one article came up about your city. I mean zero."

"That's no surprise; we don't believe in modern technology and lifestyles."

"We?" Tahira's head tilts.

"I mean them." Cadell pauses and reflects, "A Missionary came to *Night Harbor* and spoke to us about life outside of *Covingo District*. This fascinated my parents. We've been four years free of their bondage. However, recently we heard that things have been changing with congregants marrying outsiders. They're being taught new *ways* of living. We're hoping for change for all the congregants. That's why my parents visit there often."

"Are they planning on returning there to live?"

Cadell nods. "Definitely."

"Do you think you'd ever go back?"

"Only if my wife would accompany me," he winks at her.

"I'm your future wife. I'll go wherever you go."

"I couldn't have asked for a better wife."

Wherever my husband goes, I'll go. It may take getting used to, but that's part of being a Missionary. Embracing new cultures. Really sad to have had to postpone joining #EnfuegoMissions, but I'll go one day.

16

Around 11:30PM, Tahira's phone vibrates on the dashboard of Cadell's car.

She picks up. "Hi Vassos. Of course she can stay with me again. Are you going to propose? Yayyyy!! I'm going to Greece. I'm going to Greece. Yeah Cadell's here. He's dropping me off. I'll message you when I get inside."

"Wipe that grin off your face," Cadell yells when she hangs up.

"Excuse me?"

"Who was that?"

"Didn't you hear me say *Vassos*? My friend from work," Tahira quips.

"Oh, you all are friends now?"

"I thought you liked him? We double dated with him and Olympia last summer."

"I don't CARE," Cadell responds enraged.

"What's going on Cadell?"

"You're spending too much time with that man; friend or not."

"He has a girlfriend, who you've met. There's nothing going on between us," she states not understanding his behavior.

"I don't like the idea of my fiancée hanging out with another man."

"Is this how you're going to be throughout our marriage? Jealous of every man who speaks to me?"

"I'm not jealous, but I'm on to their tactics," Cadell grits his teeth.

"You sound crazy."

"I want you to stop seeing him."

"I'm not *seeing* him," Tahira laughs. "We're friends. Coworkers. He knows I am engaged. He's going to propose to his girlfriend when she returns. That's why he called. He wanted me to help him plan their engagement."

"You're not making this easy for me Tahira. I'm trying to remain calm."

"It's cute that you're jealous, but there's nothing going on between me and Vassos."

"You don't care about my feelings?"

"Why are you trying to isolate me from everyone? At this rate you may as well ask me to be a housewife and live in a cabin in the woods."

"That sounds perfect," Cadell replies.

"You're kidding right?"

Cadell turns his gaze from Tahira mashing the brakes hard in fury. "Yes Tahira."

"Slowwww down. Are you trying to kill us?"

17

On Sunday morning Tahira headed to her fiancé's workplace.

"How much are you betting today?" Siren inquires, when Tahira sits at the bar.

"$100."

"Want a drink?"

Tahira glances at the menu. "I'll have the house special."

"You're sure you want to take such a risk? That's a strong drink."

"I am in a casino. It's all about risks," Tahira winks.

"You've changed so much since we first met."

"Good or bad?"

"I'm not sure. I admired your innocence," Siren says mixing the drink.

"Not so innocent anymore."

"You all had sex?" she gasps.

"He said that's for marriage."

"That's his beliefs?"

"Yup. We mainly kiss and hold hands. We go no further. He respects me and is also a virgin."

Siren laughs boisterously. "Get out of here with that nonsense. Don't let him lie to you. You seem like a smart girl. Do you see how **hot** he is? Do you really believe that he's a virgin?"

"Yes I do," Tahira declares. "He is a Christian. Even though you don't believe it. Plus his culture is against pre-marital sex. He is very cultural."

"Didn't peg you for a dunce."

I am no dunce. I have to believe him. He said he's a virgin. WAIT. What if he lied?

Cadell marched up to Tahira during his mid-morning break. "You need to stop speaking to her. She's going to corrupt your mind."

"Isn't she your friend?"

"Coworker, not friend. I don't like her. Every time you speak to her you always have a question for me. I can see it in your eyes. What do you want to know?"

"Are you a virgin? Don't pinch me either. Answer the question."

"She made you question my virginity?"

"Answer the question Cadell."

"Yes, I am Tahira. Nothing to hide and I am not ashamed," Cadell replies smugly.

"Good."

"Have you and your mom discussed the menu?"

"Shouldn't we be doing that?"

"I've left the planning all to you. I'm just the money man. Paying for it. Business is going well and I've gotten my debt down to $1.8 million."

He kisses her forehead.

"That's awesome babes. We have a few months left, with that amount of decrease you could be debt free before our wedding day."

"That's the plan."

"I wish Kaiora was here to plan with me. She'd have loved this," Tahira sighs.

"You need true friends. She's not what you need in your life as a best friend. Your best friend should be someone who would stand by you. As matter of fact I am your best friend."

"The bestest," she blushes.

Five days later Tahira goes to her parents' house to ask for their opinion about a wedding gift for Cadell.

"Where's dad?" Tahira asks hastily.

"Men's All Night Prayer Meeting," Tahiti answers.

"The Elders take their roles as leaders seriously."

"Amazing isn't it? Hopefully he's praying about giving you a break concerning your wedding. His ways are too old-fashioned."

"Do you think he'll walk me down the aisle?"

"Of course, he's your father."

"But, he doesn't like Cadell," Tahira states tensely.

"Don't worry your pretty head off about that sweetie. Think happy wedding day thoughts. Really nice of your fiancé to pay for everything."

"He said you and I can plan everything."

"Oh chile, you know your momma was going to do that anyway."

"Yes, mom. I know," Tahira giggles.

18

On Saturday Tahira joined Vassos for brunch.

"What is her favorite color?" Tahira inquires.

"Uh, pink?"

"You're guessing?"

Vassos stares at Tahira perplexed, "What does this have to do with my proposal? I thought I just had to get down on one knee and ask her to marry me?"

"You asked for my help. Don't insult my craft. Besides, you can't do my girl like that. She'll have only one proposal. It must be super special."

"By help I meant you taking photos."

"Hmph!! Well Vassos, if you're going to propose in Fortazonio, you have to do it our style."

"Okay, okay," he shakes his head, "women."

"That's right. Shall we continue? So on that day…" Tahira begins to rattle off a to-do list for Vassos.

Cadell parks his car and heads to the ATM. He didn't expect to see his fiancée and her so called *friend* laughing and smiling at one another in the restaurant next door.

He storms into the restaurant and bursts out, "In plain sight huh?"

"Hi honey. Whatcya doing here?" Tahira runs to give him a kiss.

Cadell glances at Vassos. "I should be asking you the same question. Are you on a DATE with this man? You got some nerve Tahira. Cheating on me in plain sight."

Tahira rolls her eyes. "Oh. My. Gosh. Here we go again. Will you come off it? No one's cheating. I am helping Vassos plan his proposal to Olympia."

"He doesn't have any other friends?" Cadell barks indignantly.

"Don't be rude."

"I'm going to go. Looks like you all need to talk. Call you later Tahira." Vassos looks at Cadell. "I mean no disrespect man. She was only helping me out."

"Why do you always do this? Embarrass me?" Tahira cries when Vassos leaves.

"Oh, I'm the one embarrassing you? You're out here laughing it up with another man and I'M EMBARRASSING YOU?" Cadell huffs.

"Keep your voice down," she motions, trying to dodge the prying eyes of the other guests. "I thought you don't like to make scenes?"

"This scene is all your creation. You and your lil Greek boyfriend. I know he's appealing to you because he's a foreigner. You just *love* other cultures."

"Vassos and I are JUST FRIENDS. I feel like a broken record. I don't like reiteration. Do you want me to say it in Greek?"

"Are you mocking me?"

"No Cadell. We're having a pointless conversation because of your insecurity."

"I'm telling you Tahira, watch yourself."

"Why? Are you going to pinch me? Am I *misbehaving*? I'm going home to call *MY FRIEND*." Tahira pushes her chair out. "Enjoy the rest of your evening."

Cadell punches the wall upon entry into his house. He goes to the kitchen sink and washes off the blood from his hand.

"What happened to your hand?" Cyra asks entering the kitchen.

"What are you doing here?"

"Never mind that, what happened?"

"I'm trying my hardest NOT to lose my cool. That man is messing up my relationship and plans. I see him slickly making his way into Tahira's heart under the guise of friendship."

She hands him a paper towel. "Vassos?"

"Yes. I was cool before, but now he's infiltrating my territory. Calling her. Taking her out. They're spending a lot of time together. It's like I don't even exist. He's become her new best friend. THAT SHOULD BE ME," Cadell complains.

"Don't worry; I'll get rid of him."

19

Monday after work, Tahira met with her mother and future mother-in-law for her dress fitting.

Tahira rolls her eyes at her fiancé. "Do you have to be here? You're not supposed to see my dress before the wedding day. Isn't it cultural faux pas?"

"Your tone. Watch it."

Tahira rubs her arm. "My skin is red."

"You'll be fine," Cadell mocks. "I'm not staying. My mom will be representing me in today's fitting. To ensure that whatever you choose is appropriate for our family coming from overseas. Nothing about my wedding day should insult them."

"You mean *our* wedding day?"

"Same thing."

"No need for an attitude."

"There she is. Bye baby." Cadell waves her off.

Why does he always dismiss me? This can't be what relationships are about. My father has never disrespected my mom. Dad treats mom like a Queen. I feel like a child. Would you cut it out? Stop thinking negative about your relationship. Every relationship is different. This is what I get for marrying into another culture. I must respect my fiancé's culture.

"My in-law you look stunning in that dress," Cyra coos.

"I don't particularly like it. Mom, what do you think?"

Tahiti wrinkles her nose in disagreement, "No honey. That's not it."

Tahira walks back into the fitting room.

Cyra glares at Tahiti. "What's wrong with the dress?" she mumbles. "It's modest and lovely."

"It makes her look old," Tahiti responds.

"You new age moms don't understand modesty."

"*New Age?* Why are you speaking like that? She is **my daughter** and this is her only wedding day. I want her to look gorgeous and age appropriate. No disrespect to your culture. Evangelist Cyra, your behavior has changed since my daughter got engaged to your son. Are you having second thoughts about their upcoming nuptials?"

"No, no. I'm still learning your culture that's all. I have no daughters of my own and I am happy to share in this experience. It's all new to me so I'll take whatever advice you give. I know my son will be happy either way. You have a beautiful daughter."

"Glad that we're on the same page. Next dress honey," Tahiti calls out to her daughter.

The Manantes' House

"How was the dress fitting my love?"

"Tahiti is incorrigible. You should've seen what she wanted to put our son's future wife in. So much skin showing," Cyra grimaces.

"Was it a short dress?"

"No Quintos. But, I wanted a turtleneck long-sleeved ball gown and they pretty much laughed at me. The congregants from back home would have a fit if she's seen in anything that shows more than her face and hands. You know our culture."

"What do you want me to do?"

"GET RID OF HER MOM," Cyra tells her husband. "The best friend wasn't an issue, but we need Tahira in total isolation. She can't have friends. Friends influence, good or bad. These females of Fortazonio are too modern for my liking."

"No problem my love, I'll get rid of her."

20

Tahira buried her head in the pillow as the news pierced her heart. **Vassos is dead.** At least that is the news she received from both his girlfriend and their boss. It seemed like just yesterday they were discussing plans for his proposal to Olympia. She couldn't imagine life getting any worse. First, her best friend ended their friendship. Now, her new friend was dead. There was no explanation for what was happening. Something was off and she felt it strong, but couldn't put two and two together.

It took Tahira a while to notice that someone was at the door. She opened it with red puffy eyes.

"Why are you sad my love?"

"It's Vassos. He's d-dead," Tahira cries onto Cadell's shoulders.

"Are you sure?"

She wipes her face. "I just got the news. Apparently it was a hit and run outside of his apartment."

"Do they know who did it?"

"Olympia ensured me that they're investigating. Her father is the leader of the *Naval Investigation Unit*. They're not going to rest until his killer is found."

"What if it was an accident?" Cadell consoles his fiancée.

"Olympia would never accept that as an explanation. She thinks he was murdered."

"Why would she come to that conclusion?"

"It doesn't matter. I support her in her decision. When I meet his killer, I'll ask why. Why kill an innocent man?"

21

A week after Tahira heard the news about Vassos' death, she responded to her mother's messages inviting her to dinner.

While on their way to the mall, Tahira zones out.

Suddenly she hears a voice. **Pray.**

"Mom, did you say something?"

"No, honey."

The voice repeats. **Pray Tahira pray.**

Tahira ignores the voice.

What do I need to pray for?

"So honey, what restaurant are we going to?" Tahiti makes a left turn.

"Mom, look out—"

An hour later, Ramiro paces the hallway of the hospital.

The doctor emerges from Tahiti's room, "There's been an accident Mr. Zagori. Your wife has been severely injured. She is in a coma."

"My daughter?"

"Minor bruises. We're keeping her for observation," the doctor continues,

"Would you like to see her now?"

"Yes," Ramiro chokes.

Tahira lay on the bed hooked up to an IV. Her father walks in the room with tears in his eyes.

With a weakened voice, Tahira tries to speak. "D-d-d-dad. I----"

"Don't speak honey. It's not your fault."

She motions for him to hand her the phone lying on the nearby table. Tahira types some words and hands the phone to her father.

"*The Holy Spirit prompted me to pray, but I ignored HIM. This is my fault. Is mom dead?*" Ramiro looks up from the phone. "My daughter, this isn't your fault. Your mom isn't dead, but in a coma. This is an attack on our family. You can't expect to be praying like the Elders and I have for all these months and not expect attacks. I will pray until those people leave our lives and are exposed for the liars they are."

Tahira types again and hands the phone back to Ramiro.

"*Dad, don't speak like that about my fiancé and his family. They are nice people.*" Ramiro holds his daughter's hand. "It's okay Tahira. I'm going to continue fighting for this family. No devil is going to kill my family."

After his visitation with his daughter, Ramiro goes into his wife's hospital room; the sight of her lying helplessly on the bed made his heart sink.

The tears pour out of his eyes as he lay next to Tahiti. "Look at what these wicked people did to you. A coma. Oh honey, you should've listened to me. You opened a door of destruction into our household. But, I will fight it."

22

"How is your mother doing?"

"She is still in her coma, Mrs. Manantes," Tahira cries. "It's been 3 long months. My dad's been by her side every day. I go by to help him with cooking and household chores."

"How is your father? Is he weakened at all by this? I know these things take a toll on men."

"My dad is a fighter, ever since I was a baby and almost died. He said he made it his business to ensure that I fulfill God's purpose for my life."

Cyra holds Tahira's hand. "Are you sure you don't want to be with your family? We're almost finished with the wedding plans."

"I want to be here. As a matter of fact my father told me that I should get to know you all better. Spend time around you so I know what I am getting myself into."

"That's shocking."

"Why?"

"He treats us well in Church and has been kind to me and my husband, but I know he doesn't particularly like our son."

"He has come around," Tahira smiles weakly.

"Will your father still be joining us later for dinner?"

"Yes, we'll both be there."

"What is it my love?" Quintos asks Cyra while he prepared the night's meal.

"It's not the best friend, the coworker, or the mother. The FATHER is the problem. Even though we have Tahira where we want her, her father still has influence over her. When I try to control him, I can't. He's STRONGER than me. All those men in the congregation are getting stronger the more they have their all night prayer meetings. I feel weak around them."

"Do you want me to do something about him?"

"No, let's wait and see how much longer he could endure," Cyra chortles. "Eventually his wife will die. And there's nothing like death to weaken a man's defenses."

"Your call. Soon we'll be home."

"Yes, as soon as Cadell marries his beautiful bride." Cyra smiles maniacally as she set the table.

23

November 20th signified exactly 2 months until Tahira and Cadell's nuptials. Her in-laws invited her father to dinner as they prepared for the upcoming union of the families.

"Dad, thanks for coming to the Manantes' with me. Even though I know you don't like Cadell."

"I support you Tahira. I know you won't marry him."

"We are getting married in eight weeks."

"Only if you say **I Do** will I believe it. Until then I will be praying against it. My only daughter has to marry a True Man of God, not a counterfeit."

"Why do you keep questioning his relationship with Jesus?"

"I'm not questioning anything. I know for a fact that Cadell is a fraud," Ramiro answers.

"Let's go dad. Please BEHAVE tonight."

"Good night Elder Zagori. Welcome to our home," Quintos greets.

"Mr. Manantes. Mrs. Manantes. Thank you," Ramiro retorts politely.

"What about your wife? How long does she have to live?" Cyra blurts out.

"What my wife meant to say is… How is your wife?" Quintos covers, glaring at his wife.

"I will answer your question Mrs. Manantes," Ramiro asserts. "My wife is going to be fine. Being in a coma doesn't mean she is on her deathbed. I am praying and as long as I am praying there is hope."

Tahira looks at Cadell nonplussed. "Can't we leave them to have dinner alone?"

Cadell rubs her hand, "Baby let's sit. Our parents will work out their drama."

"Your food smells good Mrs. Manantes," Tahira compliments.

"You should start calling me mom. When you marry my son you'll be my daughter."

"Why would she call you *mom*? You're not her mother."

"DAD!" Tahira shouts.

"Dinner is served. Let's eat," Mr. Manantes announces.

Ramiro stops him. "You forgot to pray."

"No dad, they don't—"

"Excuse me? They don't what? **Pray**?" Ramiro scratches his head in disbelief. "You can't be serious. A Christian family who doesn't **pray**? What is going on here?"

Cadell speaks up offended at Mr. Zagori's distaste for his *culture*. "This is what we practice in our family. We believe in *one prayer covers all*. Our morning devotions cover all prayers for the day."

"I see. What exactly do you all do during your *morning devotions*?" Ramiro probes.

"That's not your business," Cyra snaps.

"Actually Mrs. Manantes, it is my business. If my daughter is going to marry your son I need to be aware of his background."

"Are you judging our beliefs?" Quintos states angrily.

"Tell me what they are," Ramiro continues. "It just dawned on me; you come to church only on Sundays. None of you participate in worship. Only Cadell plays the piano. Mr. Manantes you said you're a Prophet yet I've **never** seen you operate in your office since you've started attending our church almost two years ago. Neither you nor your son comes to Men's All Night Prayer…"

Cadell's pulse starts to race. "Are we being interrogated in our own home?"

"I'd like you to explain to me what kind of scam you're all trying to pull. What did you learn in *Night Harbor*? What church did you come from? Who is your 'leader'? Because I don't believe you are Christians at all. Different culture or not. Every Christian share similar foundational beliefs; and **praying** more than once a day is one of them."

"Is that what this is all about? You want to **pray** before your meal?" Cadell seethes.

"I taught my daughter the ways of the Lord and I would like the man she is going to marry to follow the same beliefs she grew up on. As far as I see you're no *Priest of the household*. How could you lead my daughter and you don't even have a relationship with Jesus?"

"You can't judge my relationship," Cadell responds defensively.

"Then say HIS name."

"Dad, can I speak to you outside? NOW!!" Tahira demands.

"WHY? WHY? Why are you trying to hurt me? Is it because of mom? I understand that you're emotional, but HOW DARE YOU ATTACK

MY FIANCE AND HIS FAMILY? That's not fair. Control your emotions. You're not acting Christ-like at all," Tahira screams frantically on the Manantes' front porch.

"Tahira, I am begging you to open your eyes to see truth before you get hurt."

"Are you threatening me?"

"We're in a battle and I need you to open your spiritual eyes to what is happening," Ramiro pleads with his daughter. "That family is deceiving you. I know what I am saying."

"Dad you know what, you need to leave. You're behaving like a lunatic. I know you're not thinking clearly because your wife is in a coma."

"You don't even respect me anymore. They've turned you against me."

"Dad, just go…" Tahira sniffles.

Tahira walks back into the house apologizing to Cadell and his parents. "I'm sorry for my dad's behavior. He's going through a lot since my mom has been in her coma."

"It's okay my daughter. Everything will be fine. You need to focus on your upcoming wedding to my son," Cyra soothes.

Cadell hugs Tahira. "It's going to be alright baby. Your father will get the help he needs."

Tahira begins sobbing uncontrollably in his arms.

24

Ramiro picks up his Bible and heads for the door. "Are you coming to service this morning?"

"My cake tasting is today."

"You've missed five weeks already. That's not good. Why can't your tasting happen after service is over?"

"I'm covered in that department. I pray and read my Bible. I've downloaded audio sermons to listen to in my car," Tahira answers nonchalantly.

Ramiro breathes in. "Soon you'll be telling me you're praying only once a day." He slams the door behind him.

"You're here five Sundays in a row. Are you sure you won't get struck down for coming to a casino on *The Lord's Day*?"

"Hardy, har, har, Siren. I can praise Jesus from anywhere. Don't need to attend Church services to do that."

"No need to explain anything to me. You've changed so much, it's shocking."

"Still can't decide if it's good or bad?"

Siren shakes her head. "It's bad. Your innocence is completely gone.

Even though you said you and Cadell haven't had sex, your aura is tainted."

"If I wanted to be judged I have my dad for that. Cadell and I are going to our cake tasting."

"You're actually going through with that **sham** of a wedding?"

Tahira blinks frenziedly. "Sham? How could you say that Siren? I thought you don't get involved in your coworkers' business?"

"You're not my coworker. I don't want to see you get hurt. I've seen this situation played out before. Innocent girl getting led astray by some pretty boy actor."

"He's not an actor. Thanks for your concern, but I can handle myself. I'm almost 23 years old," Tahira snaps.

"23 don't make you a grown woman baby girl. Slow your roll. Make sure to think about what you're doing before you walk down the aisle, because divorce is UGLY." She pours a drink for a customer.

"Who's talking about divorce?" Tahira whispers.

"Do you all have a prenup?"

"Why? Prenups are for persons who want an escape plan. Cadell and I love one another."

"Same thing I thought. Why do you think I ended up working here?" Siren says walking away to mix a drink.

She was married? I wonder if she was that innocent girl. Anyways I don't care. No one is going to stop me from marrying the love of my life. I am soon going to be Mrs. Cadell Manantes.

"Which flavor do you prefer Tahira?" Cadell points at the samples later that morning.

"You choose. I'm not fussy about cake. Have you finalized our honeymoon destination?"

"Yes."

"Where are we going?"

"Mt. Thafivin," he reveals flatly.

"Your home country?"

"Why so glum?"

"I wanted to go to Lux Point Milano," Tahira whimpers.

"Maybe another time. It's part of our culture to start off our married life in our home country. From the moment we say *I do* everything changes."

"What do you mean by *everything*?"

"Not to worry. You'll be happy with our life."

This is not how I envisioned my engagement period. Every day things seem to be closing in on me. I feel like I am choking.

25

At the end of the tasting, Tahira begins to tug at Cadell's shirt. "I feel stifled; like I can't breathe."

"Do you need to go to the hospital?" he asks worried.

"I mean all this. I think we're moving fast. I don't know if I can embrace your culture. It's too much."

"Are you having second thoughts about our marriage?"

"It's more than that. Look at me, I'm getting ready to walk down the aisle and my mom is in a coma," Tahira cries.

"I can understand that you have cold feet. And I know how important your mom is to you," Cadell says.

Tahira stands up. "It's not cold feet. The more we plan, the more I am finding out details about you and your culture that I don't like."

"You're ashamed of me and my culture?"

She shakes her head, "You don't get it."

"Help me to understand."

"I don't know how to explain it."

"You're telling me this a few weeks before our wedding?" Cadell asks exasperated.

"Better now than when we stand at the altar."

"I don't know what is happening with you Tahira, but its cause for concern. I thought you were happy."

"I am happy, but I can't ignore how I feel. Can you honestly tell me that we know enough about one another to get married?"

"We have a lifetime to learn about each other. What I do know is that I love you and I would do anything for you."

"That sounds cute and all, but something is off."

Not liking where the conversation was headed Cadell gives her an ultimatum. "You need to go home and think about this. You're going to throw away our relationship because of feelings? Everyone has cold feet before they get married."

"I need space. I'm going to go take the bus. I'll call you when I am ready." Tahira begins to walk out of the bakery.

"I can drive you home."

"It's okay."

"Tahira, WAIT!"

"Get off of me Cadell, I said I'M TAKING THE BUS!"

26

How long do I have to wait on this bus? Uggh! Why didn't I drive my car?

A woman comes and sits next to Tahira smiling. "Hi."

"Hi."

"How are you doing?"

"Sorry miss, I'm not in the mood for small talk," Tahira responds flippantly.

The woman looks at Tahira's engagement ring. "Getting married soon?"

"What is it to you?"

"You don't look happy."

"That's none of your business," Tahira retorts angrily.

"You should be happy, unless you're marrying the wrong person."

"What do you mean?"

"The man you're about to marry isn't your husband."

"You don't know anything about me or my fiancé."

"Are you happy in your relationship?"

Tahira begins to get irritated. "No relationship is perfect."

"That doesn't answer my question."

"Why should I answer you? I don't even know you," Tahira snaps at the woman.

"Are you happy? If not, don't marry him."

"Lady, I'm trying to be nice, but buzz off."

"Ok Tahira, you were warned. Cadell is NOT your husband." The woman gets up and walks away.

"WAIT, how—"

What on earth? How'd she know my name? How does she know Cadell? Who is she and why do I need a warning?

27

January approached faster than Tahira thought. It was the Monday before her January 20th wedding and she went to her in-laws' for family time.

"Good night my daughter. Come in. Cadell will be here shortly. Make yourself at home. I'll be in the kitchen."

"Thanks Mrs. Manantes."

"You should start calling me mom," she replies heading to the kitchen.

Walking over to the fireplace mantel Tahira notices a book labeled **Manantes Book of Missions.**

This looks like their Missions diary.

She takes the book and sits down on the sofa.

OFFICE OF THE LEADER

HQ: Covingo District, Night Harbor, Mt. Thafivin

OFFICIAL DOCUMENT

Greetings to the Congregants of **Agaitimo**. This booklet gives you an overview of our beliefs. The full manual is locked away in our HQ Library. We wouldn't want our secrets getting into the wrong hands. Please be warned NOT to leave this booklet lying around.

As you know, in the Christian Bible in the book of Timothy 3:1-5 it states,

But mark this: There will be terrible times in the last days. People will be lovers of themselves, lovers of money, boastful, proud, abusive, disobedient to their parents, ungrateful, unholy, without love, unforgiving, slanderous, without self-control, brutal, not lovers of the good, treacherous, rash, conceited, lovers of pleasure rather than lovers of God— having a form of godliness but denying its power. Have nothing to do with such people.

This Christian religion has long tried to control mankind. And therefore it was our Founders who decided to go against this Timothy character (hence our name **Agai**timo) and create our own perfect society and world. What is wrong with self-love? If you don't love yourself first, then who will? Who can love you more than you? What's wrong with loving money? Money brings joy and allows people to buy whatever they need. Why should we suffer?

It is important that we stay under the radar. That is why we do not allow technology or any advanced equipment in *Covingo District*. Information about us will not be available on the internet. Persons may only come into our society invited. The following is a brief description on how we conduct our *Missions*. Please note that detailed information is available in the manual.

- Though we don't adhere to the Christian belief of rules and control, it is important to have a <u>structure</u> for our congregants to follow.

1. Some will call us a cult, but we are not. Our city is filled with beautiful rich people. Congregants are either born wealthy or marry into wealth. Looks are important. Therefore, Congregants MUST have beautiful spouses.

2. Our title, monetary influences and mind control is what helps us accomplish our goals. Our goal is to eradicate all the *ugly poor* people on this planet. Not by killing, but simply marrying our kind. Eventually the world will be full of rich beautiful people.

3. All Controllers on Missions MUST work in the Finance industry. How they do it is up to them. While on Missions they MUST present a service to beautiful people of the *Missions City* so that they could get wealth. Requirements: Service users MUST come to *Covingo District*. The Controller is responsible for convincing the *subjects* to move to *Covingo District*. Upon entering into *Covingo District*, *subjects* undergo a deactivation process. This is done without their knowledge.

4. Controllers can use any form of religion as a cover for their *Missions*. Since Christianity is popular and a fast growing religion, Controllers are asked to choose that religion. However, it is their choice.

5. Controllers who choose Christianity as their *Missions Cover* MUST attend 1 service a week, but CANNOT participate in their Worship. Controllers however, can play instruments (music is art) and speak a language learned to confuse Christians and not blow their cover. Controllers are also required to become the Leader of a Youth Ministry. As the Leader the Controller is required to subtly indoctrinate the young men (only the good looking ones) and convince them to come to *Covingo District*. These unknowing participants will undergo the male deactivation process and become *Controllers*. (See Manual Section 1-5 for further information).

6. "Prayer" is to happen once a day during **Morning Devotions**. Morning Devotions is a time where *Controllers* and their families recite the pledge and anthem of **Agaitimo.** This will help them throughout the day on their quests.

7. *Controllers* sent out for Missions are required to go with *Parents*. *Parents* are couples in our society who cannot have their own biological children. We do not shun these men and women, but embrace and reward them for a greater cause. No *Controller* is allowed to go on *Missions* with his birth parents. (See Manual Section 1-7 for further information).

8. *Parents* MUST adopt a "spiritual" title of whatever religion the *Controller* chooses to use for his *Missions*. It is the *Controller's* responsibility to choose titles for his *Parents*.

9. *Parents* are to choose beautiful wives for their "sons". A son CANNOT choose his own wife. If a son is unable to convince a *subject* (woman) to marry him, he HAS to pay the ultimate penalty. However, if a *Parent* decides he should be given another chance then they will be brought before the Leaders to plead their case. New *Parents* would then be assigned.

10. *Controllers* are allowed to use ANY means necessary to get a *subject* to marry him. Words of affection, etc. SEX is NOT allowed before a *Controller* marries a *subject*. (See Manual Section 1-10 for further information).

11. Anyone close to a *subject,* who the *Parents* deem as a threat, MUST be **outed**. (See Manual Section 1-11 for further information).

12. EMCW (**Electronic Mind Controlling Waves**): The initial stage of any *Missions* is hard work and daunting. It is up to the *Controller* to train his *subject* to be submissive. Therefore the *Controller* is allowed to formulate his own way of implanting the EMCW. This can be done by using subtle tactics, such as ***pinching***. The *Controller* would implant himself with the microscopic device created by our Founder, and whatever method he uses, the *subject* would then reconsider her response. Example: If she becomes too curious about the *Controller* he can *pinch* her so that she changes her mind. Whatever the *Controller* says to her after, she would agree. Or if it's an argument she would see his side. EMCW leaves the *subject* with zero control of her thoughts. Once as she is mentally where the *Controller* wants her then he has no further need for

the EMCW. The EMCW can and SHOULD be applied when necessary...

Tahira begins to shudder as the revelation hit her. Not wanting to spend a minute longer in the now eerie household, she drops the manual and runs for her life.

"Where are you going?" Cyra looks down at the open booklet and gasps.

28

Cyra paces back and forth as she waits for Cadell. Seeing Tahira run out of the house and the open booklet could only mean one thing, they HAD to do damage control. She could not endure another *Mission* with Cadell, he'd proven to be the hardest *Controller* yet.

Cadell bursts through the door in a rage. "What is it that you want? My phone's been ringing nonstop."

"Look around, what do you see?"

"Is this a trick?"

"WHAT DO YOU SEE?" she yells.

"A booklet—" Cadell looks at Cyra. "Oh no, she didn't…"

"EVERY SINGLE WORD."

"How do you know she read it?"

"The haste that she left in and the open booklet. How could you be so STUPID and leave the book out?" Cyra scolds.

"Why are you blaming me? I'm not the only member of this family. Besides, I don't even live here. Are you sure it wasn't you or your husband?"

"Watch your tone."

"You're not my mother."

Cyra slaps Cadell. "I am your mother. At least until this *Mission* is over. Have you forgotten that you're the one who has us in this mess in the first place?"

"Leave Zerenia out of this. She wasn't ready for marriage," he replies heatedly.

"You were an **amateur** *Controller* then. I fought for you to get another chance, remember. Anyways, we don't have time to argue. GO FIND YOUR FIANCEE AND CONVINCE HER TO GO THROUGH WITH THE WEDDING. TIME IS RUNNING OUT."

Cadell knew damage control was inevitable in this situation, so he immediately drove to Tahira's house.

"I don't want to talk," she responds after his knock.

"Let me in. You know how I feel about making a scene."

Tahira opens the door indignantly. "WHO ARE YOU?"

"I am Cadell Manantes, your fiancé."

"The wedding is OFF," Tahira barks. "I don't know what kind of CRAZY manipulative stunts you and your *Parents* are trying to pull, but I WILL NOT be a part of it. It all makes sense now. The pinching. The words. EVERYTHING. It makes sense. What is Agaitimo?"

Cadell bursts out laughing. "You read my dad's manuscript for his upcoming book."

"A book? Cadell, you're not going to *control* your way out of this one."

"You've spent almost two years with me. Do you really think that I'd belong to a cult?"

"So you admit it is a cult that you're a part of?"

Cadell shakes his head. "What I am saying is my dad is writing a book using some of the experiences that we had in *Night Harbor* mixed with his creative skills. Most of what you read in that booklet is called **creativity**."

"You think I'm stupid? You want to pinch me to change my mind?"

"That makes no sense. Come on, mind control? You're not thinking rationally," he jeers.

"Don't do that. You're trying to control me right now. With your words. WOW, you're really good."

"Baby, I love you. I'm not sure when doubt crept in your mind about us, but I will do whatever it takes to marry you. You are the love of my life. Don't you see how much I love you?" Cadell confesses.

"This isn't about love."

"I wanted to wait until our rehearsal dinner to tell you this... I am officially *debt free*. I've quit working at the casino and closed down my business. I don't want to do that line of work anymore. I have to start thinking like a husband."

"You're debt free?" Tahira's eyes extend. "Then you do love me. You knew how important it was to me that we start off our marriage on a clean slate."

"You'll still marry me?"

Tahira hugs him. "Yes. Tell your dad he's really good. He almost had me convinced that you all were a part of a cult."

"I'll tell him babes." Cadell tries to hide the relieved look on his face. "You're my love."

"I love you Cadell."

29

The excitement of her upcoming nuptials made Tahira restless.

As she stares into the mirror, Tahira smiles thinking about saying 'I Do' to Cadell. Their relationship was no walk in the park, but she'd long let go of the typical cookie cutter experience she'd heard others had. Her life was no **Hallmark** movie and she had to accept it. Cadell was a great man and his future path was parallel to hers, this was what mattered. She brushed any negative feelings aside as *cold feet*.

"Are you ready?"

Tahira beams at her future mother-in-law with her petite frame and loosely curled auburn hair. Cyra donned an indigo satin frock. "Yes mom, I am."

"My son chose well."

"Do you Tahira Zagori take this man as your lawfully wedded husband, to have and to hold…"

"I Do," Tahira responds excitedly before the minister could finish talking.

"And do you Tavario Mikos take this woman as your lawfully wedded wife, to have and to hold…"

"I Do."

Tahira's eyes shift between the minister and Tavario. "Where's Cadell?"

"Who's Cadell?" Tavario asks her.

Tahira jumps out of her bed in a cold sweat. It was *1:44AM* on January 18th. The room begins to spin as she realizes that the man in her heart was still Tavario. This was not a good sign.

Waking up early for breakfast was a chore for Tahira. She hadn't gotten much sleep.

Putting down her cup of *Lavender Milk*, Tahira stands akimbo.

Think Tahira think. How can I marry Cadell when another man is in my heart?

"Dad, how is mom doing? Any signs of coming out of her coma before my wedding?" Tahira asks a few hours later.

"I am still praying for your mother. It's been months and her condition hasn't changed."

"I would like to speak to you about my wedding day. Are you walking me down the aisle?" she requests hoping his answer was different.

"I would love nothing better than to walk you down the aisle. However, if Cadell is the groom I can't."

"I only intend on marrying once and it breaks my heart that you're refusing," Tahira says trying to reason with her father.

"I am not going against my beliefs. If I walk you down the aisle then I am being a hypocrite. Giving a daughter away is major for a father. It means that I support your marriage and accept your fiancé as my son-in-law. I have stated from the beginning that I do not like Cadell, nor is he your husband. Why waste time?"

"I. I. I. I. I. That's all you're saying. You're being selfish. Why can't you respect my choice? You always say how much you love me and would support me, but here you are declaring that you're not going to be there for me on the MOST IMPORTANT DAY OF MY LIFE. As far as I am concerned, if you don't show up to the rehearsal dinner tomorrow, you could consider me disowned. Do not call me your daughter anymore. I do not want anything to do with you EVER AGAIN."

"Tahira—"

"No Ramiro. I am serious. You've gone too far with your hatred."

"You call me by my first name?"

"Show up tomorrow or else…"

30

Rehearsal Dinner

The previous night's argument plagued Tahira's mind. She went apprehensively to what was supposed to be a happy occasion.

The room was filled with strangers. It was now 6:45, 15 minutes until their dinner was scheduled to start and still no sign of her father. Disappointment rose in her chest as she tried to keep from crying.

Cadell scans the room. "Baby, where is your father?"

"He isn't coming," Tahira sighs.

"I know he doesn't like me, but you're his daughter. I thought for sure that he'd at least show up to support you."

"My father is an extremely adamant man. When he says **no** that's what he means." Wiping the tears from her eyes she proceeds to sit on her reserved seat.

Hitting his glass with a silver fork, Quintos takes the floor. "Ladies and gentlemen it is my pleasure to stand before you tonight as we celebrate the upcoming nuptials of my son and his beautiful fiancée, Tahira."

The room erupts with applause.

Tahira tries to smile, but remains with her head down in shame. No one was there to support her.

Cadell takes the mic from his father. "When I met this woman, I knew that she was special. The journey hasn't been an easy one, but we're here. Tomorrow we say 'I Do'. Let's raise a glass to Tahira, my love, my Queen, my everything. TO TAHIRA." Cadell raises his glass to toast.

"TO TAHIRA," the guests echo.

Cadell looks down at her, "Would you like to say anything to our guests?"

"You mean **your** guests? No one is here for me."

Sitting down he whispers in her ear, "They're here for us."

The chair screeches as Tahira gets up and runs out of the room.

"Why'd you run out on our guests like that?" Cadell questions when he catches up with her.

"STOP SAYING **OUR**."

"I am saying *our* because we're a team Tahira. Everyone is here to support us."

"Except my parents and best friend."

"Ex-best friend," he corrects.

"That's not the point," Tahira snaps. "Look at me. Tomorrow is my wedding day and I am a wreck. No parents. No friends. I didn't even have a Bachelorette Party."

"Didn't my mom throw one for you?"

"That was a Bridal Shower, it isn't the same." Tahira gazes at him, "Are you sure about us?"

"How many times are we going to talk about this? I love you."

"That doesn't answer my question. How sure are you that we're doing the right thing? Do I fit your description of a wife?"

"You've surpassed anything that I could have dreamed of. Am I not your—"

"There you two are. It is quite rude to run out on your guests like that," Cyra reprimands.

"I am sorry Mrs. Manantes," Tahira apologizes.

"You mean mom."

"Yes mom, I am sorry. I needed some air."

Cyra glances at Tahira. "You have guests. The proper protocol would have been to excuse yourself."

Cadell's eyes darts between the two women. "I know that you're trying to help mom, but Tahira's feelings are important. We were speaking, can you excuse us?"

Cyra nods. "Okay fine. But, hurry back. Tonight is all about you."

"Now where were we?"

"Let's go back outside to *our* guests. Tomorrow is our wedding day and I am happy," Tahira giggles.

"You sure you don't need a few more minutes?" Cadell probes.

"I am ready."

31

Wedding Day

It was 5AM when the alarm went off. Today was her wedding day and Tahira had mixed feelings. So much happened in the past few weeks and she couldn't grasp how to handle it. From her conversation with Siren, to the stranger at the bus stop, her dream, her father's refusal, and last night's breakdown, getting married seemed like an overwhelming experience. Soon people would be at her house helping her get ready for her day, yet none of her loved ones would be among them.

Walking downstairs in her robe, Tahira observes her surroundings. Today would be the last day she lived in this house; the house that she received as an 18th birthday present from her parents. No more sitting by the windowsill and reading her favorite novels. No more cooking in her state of the art kitchen. Instead she would be moving to a new place with her husband. That should have sent excitement through her veins, but all she wanted to do was hurl.

The doorbell rings just as her thoughts of vomiting subsided. Growing up she wanted the perfect wedding. But, with no friends to assist in the planning she had to settle for whatever was given by Cadell's family.

"Happy Birthday my daughter. This is from Cadell." Cyra hands Tahira a box. The box was beautifully wrapped in gold paper and a purple ribbon. Like a Queen's treasure chest.

"Come in. I was about to eat pizza. Do you want a slice and a cup of *Cobalt Tea?*"

"I had breakfast at home. I'm here to get you ready to meet your groom. How do you feel?"

"How is a woman to feel on her wedding day? Nervous? Nauseous? Excited? Scared? All of the above?" Tahira sighs.

Cyra plops down on Tahira's bed. "Sit, sit. Let's have a talk before your hairdresser and makeup artist comes."

"Should I open my gift now?"

"Oh yes, go ahead."

Tahira hurriedly tears open the wrapping, not caring about saving the paper. "What is it?"

"It's our family crest. We've engraved all the names of our family on it, with an addition. Welcome to the Manantes family Tahira," Cyra beams.

"I-I don't know what to say."

"Thanks will be nice."

Tahira wrinkles her nose. "I understand, but it's more of a housewarming present than a birthday present."

"You don't want to be a part of our family?" Cyra scoffs.

"I do, just expected an *actual* birthday present from him."

"You have the rest of your life to get presents from your husband. I know that this time is extremely difficult for you; getting married with your mother in a coma and your father's disapproval. My husband and I are here to represent not only Cadell, but you as well. Quintos has volunteered to walk you down the aisle."

Tahira's countenance changes to solemnity. "I wish we didn't have to talk about it. I appreciate the gesture, but he isn't my father. When the minister asks *who gives this woman away* what will he say? Legally he has no permission to do that."

"Our Leader understands the situation and has agreed to accept the condition."

"Isn't Pastor Hizaor marrying us?"

Cyra shakes her head. "You didn't hear? He cancelled last night."

"Pastor wouldn't cancel without letting me know why. Who did he call?"

Mrs. Manantes shrugs. "Cadell I guess."

Tahira tilts her head in confusion. "You *guess?*"

"Our Leader has agreed. Unless you don't think our culture is good enough."

"You can stop with the culture talk. I get it, we come from different cultures. Thanks for the *talk*. Time to get ready for my wedding."

Mrs. Manantes squeals in excitement counting down the seconds until their *Mission* was up.

32

Why did I agree to a 10 AM ceremony? I'm exhausted.

Tahira observes her silhouette in the mirror. Her dress was exquisite: A-line with a bodice that showcased her sculpted waistline; a hint of amaranth diamonds at the hem. She opted against a veil and train. All the smiles in the world couldn't erase the knots inside her stomach. This wasn't cold feet. Something was wrong and she had to speak to her fiancé.

A knock was heard on the door.

"Are you ready?"

"Mrs. Manantes, can you get Cadell? I need to speak with him."

"You cannot see the groom before your wedding."

"This is important and I'm not a traditional bride."

Cyra closes the door behind her and furiously marches down the hallway to Cadell's suite. She thought about all the possible topics of discussion. Whatever Tahira had to say couldn't be good. The ceremony was less than 5 minutes away from starting.

In a haste of fury, Cyra knocks on Cadell's door. "Tahira wants to speak to you," she blurts when he opens the door.

Cadell pauses from adjusting his tie. "Now? She's due to walk down the aisle in a few minutes."

"She insists," Cyra replies.

"I don't like this."

"Go see what she wants," she pushes him.

Removing his tie and cummerbund he exits the room heading towards the **Bridal Suite**.

"My love, what's the matter?"

"Cadell, you're a sweet man. Some may even say a *dream come true*, but not my dream." Taking off the ring Tahira picks up her dress. "I can't marry you."

"ARE YOU CRAZY?" he yells. "You're not serious."

"A few weeks ago someone asked me if I am happy."

Cadell stares at her in disbelief. "Aren't you?"

"No I'm not. When I was younger I always dreamed of marrying Tavario Mikos. He is…" She sighs. "That's the man I want to marry."

"You're dumping me because you want to marry some actor who doesn't even know you exist? You're giving up OUR RELATIONSHIP because of a fantasy?" Cadell barks.

"You wouldn't understand. When I think of my husband it's his face that I see."

"Delusional much?"

"Be that as it may, even if I never meet or marry Tavario Mikos, I know for sure that I do not want to marry you. You're not my husband. I feel it. It took a long time to realize it, but I'd rather be single and happy than married and unhappy. You, your culture, it doesn't work for me. I refuse to force myself to marry into bondage. You all may not call it a cult, but it is definitely bondage. This is the 21st century and what you all stand for is against my beliefs."

Cadell begins to exhale in fury. "You have no idea what you're saying."

"I do. Go find someone else to pinch and be a part of your crazy culture and theories."

"You're going to regret this," Cadell clenches his fists.

"The only thing I regret is not realizing this sooner. I am sure about this decision. Goodbye Cadell."

33

"Get back inside NOW!!" a uniformed man screams as Tahira exits the suite.

"Excuse me? Who are you and what are you doing outside my bridal suite?" Tahira asks not budging.

"I'm Officer Gherardi. Please get back inside."

"Officer? For what? Is something wrong?"

"Ma'am get inside, we'll speak there," the officer pleads.

Tahira stares in shock at the women standing behind him. "Olympia? Siren? What are you two doing here?"

"Let's go inside," Officer Gherardi repeats.

"Is someone going to tell me what's wrong?" Tahira queries.

"Granger Fontanez you're under arrest for the murders of Zerenia and Vassos Neizu." Officer Gherardi slams the handcuffs on Cadell's hands and proceeds to take him out of the room.

"Wait. Wait. Wait. Wait. Hold up." Tahira stands in front of the doorway, flailing her hands profusely. "Who is Granger Fontanez? Officer you have the wrong man. His name is Cadell Manantes."

The officer looks at him loathingly. "That's the name he's going by these days?"

"Olympia, what is he talking about? Cadell didn't murder anyone."

"You'll want to sit down," Olympia motions.

Tahira stops pacing and sits on the ottoman then looks at Olympia to explain the weird ordeal. "What is going on Olympia?"

Without waiting a second longer Olympia explains everything. "I am an Agent in the *Naval Investigation Unit* as was Vassos before his death. 5 years ago he received news that his sister, Zerenia, was joining something called **Agaitimo**. She came to *Jozelle Oasis,* Fortazonio as a way to rebel against her father; one of the founding members of the NIU. She did not want to be an Agent.

Before her death Zerenia contacted Vassos stating that she felt threatened and that her fiancé wasn't who he portrayed to be. They kept insisting that she had to abide by rules that she deemed archaic. Vassos paid for a flight out of the country that very night, but it was too late, the conversation was infiltrated and she was killed en route to the airport. Vassos had no doubt that it was her fiancé's doing, but he needed proof. SIGA (Starr Islands-Greece Alliance) wasn't yet formed so he had nothing to go by.

No information was found about Granger, any Fontanez' or *Covingo District* which is where Zerenia said he was from. Without any leads Vassos suffered in silence as he couldn't protect his sister from a monster. Three years ago when the alliance was formed we got word that Granger and his new *Parents* had returned. We sent an agent, Siren, to work at **Lucky Helix Casino** posing as a bartender. This was the breakthrough we'd been waiting for. Our sources in Mt. Thafivin explained to us the manual and how *Controllers* and their *Parents* operate, so Siren was able to put the pieces together about Granger and his *Missions*.

With DNA evidence collected from Granger, Siren was able to deduce that Granger Fontanez was indeed Cadell Manantes. A man wanted for murder. Vassos was sent here to get answers, but was killed in the process. Evidence was also collected to prove that Granger/Cadell killed Vassos.

Quintos and Cyra are two of the Leaders of **Agaitimo.** This was a special *Mission* for them since Granger had failed to secure a *subject* for conversion. They decided to act as his *Parents* to ensure that he completed his job aka marry a new *subject,* which in this case is you Tahira. The organization has been in existence for 25 years scamming the rich and vulnerable to build an empire. Quintos and Cyra have been arrested for murder, being an accomplice to murder, harboring a fugitive, money laundering and tax fraud. As we speak NIU Agents and members of the Royal Police Force are shutting down all operations of **Agaitimo—**"

Not being able to contain her anger, Tahira steps to Cadell's face, "How could you?"

"Tahira, you don't understand," Cadell cries out.

Tahira slaps him across the face. "There's nothing you can say. I hope you rot in jail."

The officer pulls Cadell out the door in handcuffs.

"Are you okay?" Olympia motions for Tahira to sit.

"I-I don't know what to say or think. I almost married a **murderer.** I almost got myself involved in a cult. It's too much. My wedding is ruined. My life is ruined. Who can I trust now?"

34

"Can I come in?" Tahira asks entering the hospital room.

Ramiro looks up from his newspaper to see his daughter in her wedding dress. "Happy Birthday. You married him?"

Tahira rolls her eyes, still seething that her father didn't walk her down the aisle. "How's mom?" she retorts, trying to change the subject.

"She woke up today. A miracle. Prayers answered. They transferred her to another room for observation."

"After all that happened this is the **best** news of the day."

"What happened?"

Tahira explains to her father all the details leading up to her wedding and her wedding day debacle.

"You've had quite an adventurous few months." Ramiro pauses, "I am thankful that my prayers were answered. Do you see how important it is to discern? I knew something was wrong from the start."

Tahira's eyes pops open. "Are you seriously gloating at a time like this? My life is ruined. I almost married a murderer and unknowingly almost joined a cult."

"I was praying for you for all this time," Ramiro comforts.

"You can't pray away how I feel right now. I've wasted time on a relationship that was doomed from the beginning. I was chosen by these sickos to be a part of their cult. What's the point of going to church if bad things are going to happen to me?"

"Going to church doesn't exempt you from trials and tribulations or the pains of this world, but you have hope in Jesus that *no weapon formed against you will prosper.*"

"I used to believe that. Believe in a God who cared for me and protected me from the snares of the enemy, but this isn't caring or protection. HE knew from the *Foundation of the Earth* that this would happen to me and still allowed it? How can you tell me that God loves me after HE allowed this awful situation to happen? I'm DONE."

"Tahira, let's talk about it."

"SAVE IT DAD. There's nothing you can say that would change how I feel. I'm leaving this country."

Tahira knew she wouldn't gain access into Cadell's house now that he was in jail. Her honeymoon items were in his house so she counted it as a lost. She rummaged through her closet and tossed a few items into her suitcase.

Locking the door, she walks down the stairs; dragging her suitcase to the taxi. The house her parents bought her all those years ago would be returned to them. She was ready to leave the past behind. Her early twenties were proving to be filled with angst and she wanted out.

I'm OVER all the lies, schemes, manipulations, revenge, and murders. I am traumatized and I need to get out of this country.

"FINAL BOARDING CALL. FINAL BOARDING CALL FOR ALL PASSENGERS DESTINED TO LA VIR, RUVENIVI. PLEASE PROCEED TO GATE T8…"

Part Two

1

The flight to Ruvenivi seemed longer than what was displayed on Tahira's boarding pass. Watching the luggage carousel spin made her dizzy. Finally, her purple *Royal McGovern* suitcase dropped. As she reached to pick it up, a man grabbed her from behind and pulled her close.

"Get OFF OF ME!!" Tahira screamed.

Panic set in as becoming a kidnap victim wasn't in the cards for her. Her botched nuptial was enough excitement for at least four years.

"I know this may sound weird, but can you stand still until I put on my disguise?"

The man's voice sounded familiar. However, Tahira couldn't place it.

Tahira turned around. There standing in all his fineness was the one and only **Tavario Mikos**. Tahira pinched herself. She had to be dreaming. If this was a dream she had no desire to wake up.

"I'm sorry miss. I didn't mean to startle you. My name is Tavario Mikos," he extends his hand, "what's yours?"

Instead of shaking his hand, Tahira begins to tremble, "M-my name is Tah…"

Tavario stood over her concerned. "I didn't know I still have that effect on people."

Fanning herself Tahira sits up. "W-what happened?"

"You fainted for about two minutes."

"Y-you're T-tavario Mikos," she stutters, still shocked that her dream man was inches away from her.

"That's what my birth certificate says. I didn't get your name."

"Tahira Zagori."

"Beautiful name for a beautiful woman," he smiles. "Would you like to join me for lunch? It's the least I could do."

"I'm fine."

"Please miss, I insist," Tavario replies his cheeks turning red.

Tahira stands up and brushes off invisible dust from her outfit. "Don't you have somewhere to be?"

"I'm here on vacation."

"By yourself?"

"My family will be here in a few days," he stares at her intently. "What about you? Boyfriend? Husband?"

"It's complicated," Tahira retorts trying to avoid the subject.

"I take it that means you're *single?*"

"That's none of your business," she snaps.

"Didn't mean anything by it. I doubt a beautiful woman like you would be here alone on purpose. Are you hungry?"

Words escaped her mind as she wondered what alignment happened to bring Tavario Mikos in her life; the man who she dreamed about for fifteen years. Of course he didn't know that.

Scanning the restaurant Tahira took it all in, the pristine Cathedral like décor. He'd taken her to his favorite Italian restaurant.

The waiter places a basket of Bruschetta on their table. *"Signor Mikos, sei pronto per ordinare?"*

Tavario looks at Tahira. "You can order first."

"I'll have a grilled chicken Caprese salad," she tells the waiter.

"Don't order salad if you're hungry. Feel free to eat whatever you want. The meal is on me," Tavario informs.

"It's what I want to eat."

Tavario gives the waiter his order.

"Qualsiasi sidro per te o il tuo ospite?" the waiter stood waiting to take their drink order.

"Tahira?" Tavario asks.

Tahira scans the menu and replies, "Sparkling Passion Fruit."

The waiter takes their menus and walks away.

An hour later Tahira caught herself staring at Tavario. This couldn't be real. The conversation between the two was sweet and lighthearted, as if they'd known one another forever.

"My driver will take you to your hotel," Tavario announces, at the end of their meal.

"I think you've done enough. Thanks again for lunch," Tahira expresses her gratitude.

"I want to spend time getting to know you."

"I don't think your girlfriend would appreciate that very much."

"It's complicated," Tavario mimics Tahira's earlier sentiment.

"You're an actor; I highly doubt you're single."

"We actors are humans too."

"Are you always this down to earth?"

Tavario moves a strand of hair off of Tahira's face. "Besides your faint episode, you're the first person in years who's spoken to me as a normal man."

Turning beet red Tahira giggles. "Can I be honest with you?"

"Oh no, are you a stalker?" Tavario chuckles sarcastically.

"Right now I am shocked that we're here together."

"Not accustomed to handsome men?"

"Conceited much?"

"I'm joking Tahira," he laughs. "We're friends. Lighten up."

"We don't even know one another."

"I read people really well. I have a feeling we'll be lifelong friends."

Please don't let me wake up from this dream…

2

"Here we are. Holbrook Resort & Spa," Tavario says opening the door for Tahira.

"What do you mean **we**? Is this your hotel?"

"Hey bro. You're here early," a man in a crisp black and white evening tux walks up to the duo.

"Tahira, meet August Holbrook, my sister's husband. His family owns the hotel."

August extends his hand, amused. "Pleased to meet you."

Tavario lightly punches August' shoulders. "Don't get any ideas."

Knowing exactly what their exchange meant Tahira shakes his hand. "My pleasure August."

"Let's get you checked in." He stands in front of the check-in laptop. "Well look at that. You've been upgraded to our **Princess Suite**, house special."

"That's not necessary sir. I will stick to my original booking."

August shrugs, "It's already in the system. Your room is paid in full. Any friend of Tavario is a friend of this hotel."

"Are you all serious?" Tahira looks at Tavario, puzzled.

What is happening?

Tavario winks at her. "He's the boss. Get unpacked. I'll meet you in an hour."

"Where are we off to?"

"It's a surprise," Tavario announces rolling her suitcase to the elevator.

Tahira twirls around the room in excitement and shock. Yes, this was definitely a dream she didn't want to wake up from. Sadness followed as she thought about her loved ones back home. Wishing she could share this moment with them she plops down on the bed and begins crying.

A knock on the door startles her.

"Are you ready?" the voice on the other side calls out.

Wiping her eyes she opens the door with the utmost hesitation.

"You were crying? What's wrong?" Tavario asks.

"Allergies."

"I don't believe that. Is it my bro? Have we offended you? I apologize on behalf of us both."

"You've been kind to me. I'm just having a moment."

He looks at her eagerly. "Do you want to reschedule?"

"I think you should forget you met me. I'll never be good company. It's been a tough few months."

An hour later Tahira and Tavario stood in front of majestic mountains.

"I'm glad you changed your mind."

"Tavario, it's the *Aquafire Rainbow Mountains*," Tahira beams.

"It's the only one found in the world. Imagine two mountains located next to one another. One spewing water and the other spewing fire; never affecting the land, but once every 80 days the water and fire cross paths in the air making an *Aquafire Rainbow*. Today is the 80th day for this season," he gestures dramatically at the peaks.

"It is beautiful," she cries.

"Here, I want you to have this." Tavario places a sparkly object in her hand.

"What is it?"

"I got it for you while you were unpacking; an Aquafire stone."

"This is the most beautiful jewel I've ever held."

"You're more beautiful than this jewel," Tavario compliments.

"What gives?"

"I don't follow."

Tahira places her hands on her hips. "The lunch, free room, *Rainbow Mountains*, sparkles. Is this a game you play with every woman?"

"What makes you think this is a game?"

Tahira points to the mountains. "It's too good to be true. We just met and here we are in front of the *Aquafire Rainbow Mountains*."

"I'm showing my new friend around my favorite place," Tavario answers. "Is there anything wrong with that?"

"I don't buy it. I appreciate all that you've done, but I had a horrible experience recently and my heart can't take anymore breaking."

3

The early morning waves soothed Tahira's mind as she reflected on her life for the past two years. So much had happened and she didn't know what to do next. Her life as a church girl was done. Maybe Kaiora was on to something. Christianity *is* for older folks. She tried to abide by all the rules set forth by her parents and live right according to the **Good Book**, to no avail. Bad followed her and trouble was imminent.

"There you are. I looked for you at breakfast."

"Are you stalking me?"

"More like pursuing. I was up all night thinking about you," Tavario states, standing next to her.

"What do you want?"

"Tahira, I was serious when I said I—" His cell phone rings. "Hello? I'm busy. Calm down. Now? Okay fine…" He walks off to continue his conversation.

Ten minutes later, Tavario sees Tahira sitting in the lobby.

"Can we talk?" Tavario sits down on the muted chaise lounge.

Tahira gets up, "We have nothing to speak about. I don't know you. You don't know me. Let's keep it that way."

"What's the matter?"

"I know you're an actor and have women fawning over you all the time. There was a point in my life I thought you were cool, but you're—"

"I'm sorry about earlier. An issue back home needed to be dealt with."

"You don't owe me an explanation Tavario."

"I really do want to get to know you."

"There's no need for it. You're going home soon and I'll be starting my life over. It was a dream come true meeting you, but I'm not interested." Tahira storms off.

The moonlight created the perfect ambiance for reflection. Tahira decided to take a stroll on the beach to think things through.

What is happening in my life? How do I go from engaged to single in a matter of days? I never thought my life would turn out this way. Why can't a decent man WITHOUT issues find and marry me? Am I hard to love? Is something wrong with me? Am I ugly?

4

What's all that commotion downstairs?

Tahira observes the group from the hallway balcony. It appeared that the Mikos' were officially in the building. Walking back in her room, she slams the door.

Less than a week ago I was going to be Mrs. Cadell Manantes, now I am here with my dream man who turned out to be no dream at all. I'm done with relationships. All this stress and risks, only to end up heartbroken. Cadell is a fraud and in jail. Tavario is a dream and will soon return to his reality. Complicated for him probably means his girlfriend understands that when he's away he will **play***. Who knows, celebrities are weird and live by their own rules.*

"Right this way Ms. Zagori, your party is already at the table," the waiter informs her at dinner.

"I have no *party*. I'm taking my food up to my room."

Tavario motions for her to join his family at the table and Tahira shakes her head.

"Good night Tahira, are you leaving? I've asked the waiter to send you to our table. My family wants to meet you."

"How do they know about me?"

"I told them I made a friend," Tavario smiles.

"Tavario, we aren't—"

"I know you keep trying to push me away, but I'm not going anywhere. Should I hold your hand or are you going to come willingly?"

"You're kidding right?"

He extends his hand to take hers.

"Tahira, meet my family. Family, this is Tahira."

The Mikos' all look at Tahira with the exact grin that August gave her upon their initial introduction. "Hi Tahira," they sing in unison.

Tavario begins to introduce everyone. "My parents, Evasio and Avela. My older sister Tevaia, August's wife. My other sister Teviva, her husband Hashir, and my younger brother Tavanio."

At that moment Tahira felt like the room was getting smaller. "Nice to meet you all," she smiled weakly.

"Have a seat dear," Mrs. Mikos summoned.

"I just came to say hi."

"We're friendly folks," Tevaia spoke up.

"You'll fit right in. Sit," Teviva adds.

"She's real pretty Tavario," Tevaia whispers when Tavario sits.

Later That Night

"You like my brother… Whoa be careful, I didn't mean to frighten you." Tevaia pulls Tahira from almost falling over the balcony.

"Hi Tevaia, I didn't notice you standing there. Were you saying something?"

"My brother, Tavario. I can see that you like him."

Tahira turns her gaze from Tevaia. "I don't even know him."

"I can tell. He likes you too," Tevaia beams.

"H-he does?"

"My brother only introduces women that he's serious about. You must be super special because his behavior is different."

"Good different?"

"Definitely. But I must tell you, he's going through a transition. He recently broke up with his girlfriend for a reason he hasn't yet revealed to us and is extremely vulnerable."

"Why are you telling me this?" Tahira inquires nervously.

"I like you for him. I believe you all will be more than friends. Give it time, he'll come around," Tevaia claims.

"I'm not sure what you think you're seeing now or futuristic, but a few days ago I almost got married and I'm not in any position for a relationship. As a matter of fact I've sworn off men."

"That's what we females say as a defense mechanism. Don't worry; I have faith that it'll all work out. Good night," she waves walking downstairs.

5

"Did you enjoy dinner?"

"Tavario, what are you doing out here? Shouldn't you be with your family?" Tahira gazes up at him.

"I am where I want to be. Why are you out here?"

"The ocean helps me relax."

"Want company?"

"Not really," Tahira plays with the sand.

"Ok then. Good night. Maybe I'll see you around."

"I know you're an actor, but you don't need to be dramatic around me," Tahira jokes, throwing sand at him.

"You think I'm dramatic?" he flirts, sitting down next to her.

"You're *okay*."

"I thought I was your favorite actor?"

"Hey, don't use that against me."

"Turn to face me," Tavario requests.

"What for?"

"I like looking into your eyes when we speak."

"Intense," she twitches nervously.

"You have beautiful eyes. Are you afraid to look at me?"

"I'm looking."

"Can you look without turning away?"

"I can try."

Tavario takes her hands and looks deep into her eyes as he speaks. "My life is changing and I can't explain to anyone what's happening. I had a dream and I don't know what it means. I'm battling a huge decision. Being an actor in *Vias* is a lot of pressure and sometimes I wish I could leave it all behind; but too many contracts and obligations. Why are you staring at me like that?"

Tahira pulls her hands away acknowledging her racing heart. "You said you wanted me to look at you, I can't control what my face does. Mind of its own. What was your dream about?"

"Until I know for sure, I can't share. Hope you understand."

"Tavario, you don't have to—"

"I want to kiss you right now," he pulls her in close and tilts her head.

Tahira immediately stands up. "Tavario, I can't. I **really** want to, believe me. But, I can't. You have a girlfriend."

"I don't."

"Please leave me alone. Please…"

"Wait don't run." He takes off after her.

"Join us tomorrow for our family beach day. It'll be fun," Tavario exclaims, when he catches up to her.

"Why do you assume I have nothing to do with my time?"

"I'm sorry Tahira. I shouldn't have presumed you were free. If you change your mind, meet us in the lobby at 7:30AM."

6

The next morning Tahira woke up frantic not knowing what to do. Her vacation turned out to be way more exciting than she'd ever thought. The shock of meeting Tavario in person still lingered in her cerebrum. It was 6:02AM and she hadn't decided if she would accept his offer. Did *playing hard to get* fit in with this situation? He'd been straight forward about his desire to get to know her better, but as far as she was concerned it could've been a fake; find a random woman to hang with until it was time to go home. Could she really trust him?

"Do you think she's coming Tevaia?"

"I don't know bro. We'll have to wait and see. Four minutes to go."

The family was gathered in the lobby waiting to see if Tahira had chosen to accept Tavario's invitation.

"Good morning Mikos family," Tahira announces when she arrives in the lobby.

"Hiiiiiiii Tahira," the family sings in unison. They briefly observe the awkwardness before walking off to leave the two alone.

"Wow, you look beautiful. What changed your mind?"

"Free schedule," Tahira shrugs.

"That's it?"

"What do you want from me? Blood?"

"Lighten up. You're so hostile," Tavario exclaims.

"**Not** something you say to a non-morning person."

"Come on, we have breakfast in the van."

"We're going to *Le Grand Ruvenivi Beach*. Are you enjoying breakfast?"

"I am Teviva, thank you."

In the front of the van, Avela and Evasio smiles looking at their children.

Avela whispers to her husband, "That's Tavario's wife."

"How do you know?"

"A mother's intuition."

"Avela, promise you'll stay out of it. I know you were instrumental in our daughters' spouses, but leave the boys," Evasio comments.

"They came to me. Besides, I want my sons to marry good women. Tahira is a good one. I know it. And he's going to marry her," Avela adds.

"That's between Tavario and Jesus."

"Jesus and I are great friends. I've prayed for my children to marry good people. 2 down, 2 to go."

"I hear you love, we'll see," Evasio asserts.

At lunchtime Tavario and Tahira sit by the waterfront chatting. Suddenly, a woman calls out his name.

"TAVARIOOOOO." The woman runs up to him, pushes Tahira out of the way and kisses him fervently.

Tahira stands back in embarrassment.

"What are you doing here?" Tavario asks the woman.

"Is that how you greet the love of your life?"

"We're not together anymore Nova."

"I miss you. Your reason for breaking up wasn't valid. I gave you your space; now let's work on our relationship." Nova looks around. "Where's your family?"

"They're in the restaurant having lunch."

Nova glances at Tahira. "Who's she?"

"Oh, excuse my manners. This is my friend Tahira. Tahira this is Nova, my—"

"GIRLFRIEND. I'm his GIRLFRIEND," Nova articulates. "Now shhhhh. Go away."

Tahira wipes the tears falling from her eyes. "I'm going. I got the picture loud and clear."

"That's no way to speak to anyone," Tavario reprimands.

"Sorry," Nova giggles. "Can we go eat?" She pulls Tavario and they walk off leaving Tahira standing in humiliation.

He didn't even look back.

7

Twenty minutes later Tavario walks back to where Tahira stood. "What's the matter?"

"This is your world, not mine." Tahira replies staring out into the ocean. "I've been embarrassed and humiliated enough for these past few years. What you did wasn't cool. It was immature. You're a celebrity; I'm a regular woman. Nothing would ever happen between us. I should've listened when people warned me to stay in my lane. I can't compete with a woman like Nova, she's beautiful and a model."

"Why do you think you need to compete? I told you we broke up."

"Not the way y'all kissed," she scoffs. "You didn't push her away and walked off leaving me. Look, I don't care if y'all get back together, but it's RUDE of you to walk off and leave your so called **friend**. Doesn't matter, I'll go back to the hotel and enjoy the last few days of my vacation. I'll be starting my new job soon, I don't need any distractions."

Taking her hands, Tavario looks into her eyes. "I don't want to be with her. Something is happening and she isn't..."

"Save it. Go be with your girlfriend. I'm going back to the hotel," Tahira declares walking off.

Is that the door?

Tahira turns down the volume on her phone, realizing that someone had been knocking. She walks over and opens it, surprised to see the bellhop standing with a small box in his hand.

"Good night Ms. Zagori. Mr. Mikos asked me to deliver this to you."

"Thanks, you can leave it right there," she points to the table by the door.

"He asked that you open it now."

"Okay…" Closing the door she observes the box, upset to open it, but curious.

Why does he think that he could play with my emotions?

"Can we talk?"

Nova turns her head in disdain. "What do you want with my man?"

"Nova, **stop**. We're not together anymore," Tavario corrects.

"We will get back together. This commoner certainly can't think you'd be interested in her," Nova mocks.

"Give me a minute," he says to Nova. "Tahira, let's go over there."

They walk over to the hotel entrance.

"I'm sorry to interrupt your date, but what is the meaning of this ring?" Tahira holds up the jewel.

"It's not what you think," Tavario begins to explain.

"Looks expensive. I don't want anything from you. You owe me nothing. Stop doing things for me. You have a girlfriend and I respect that."

"She's not my girlfriend."

"YET SHE'S HERE," Tahira cries. "Your family loves her."

"Nova is here on her own agenda. She had a photoshoot," Tavario explains casually.

"You don't find it odd that she's here on the same beach?"

"These things happen. It's a popular beach," he shrugs.

"Whatever, I don't care. Take back this ring."

"I don't take back gifts."

"Tavario, please. This is hard enough. I really can't do this with you."

"Do what? Be my friend?"

"We just met and I've already been introduced to your family. They're lovely. But this isn't real. You're going back to your life and I have mine."

"Keep the ring as a memory of your time in Ruvenivi," Tavario encourages. "Are you coming to the hotel's Valentine's dinner tonight?"

Tahira pauses. "It's Valentine's Day?"

"I take it you're not a fan?"

"Lost track of time. Holidays don't mean much to me anymore."

"Come tonight. I'll save you a dance," he winks.

8

"Bye Tahira," Tavario waves to her happily.

"Y-you're going?"

"My vacation is over. I have to go back and finish shooting my film. It was a pleasure meeting you. I'd like to keep in contact. Here's my number. Anytime you're in my country call me and we'll hang out."

"Are you joking right now? That's it? This is how you're leaving things?"

He stares at her. "I'm not sure what you thought was happening between us."

"Your sister said... Never mind. Unbelievable. You're nothing like I thought you were," Tahira states exacerbated.

Tavario tries to search her face for answers, "I don't understand."

"Forget it. Enjoy your life. What a waste of two weeks. You're nothing but a user."

Tavario turned out to be like Cadell; a fraud. At least I got to see his true colors. Everyone was right. Celebrities aren't like us at all...

That night Tahira decided it was time to put her heart on official **LOCKDOWN**. No more was she going to allow any man to use her for his selfish gain. All they do is pretend. Sweep her off her feet and then drop bombshells. Well no more. This was it. Her new job was to start in a few days and she was ready to face it with no distractions.

9

Nionbique, Voque

As far as world wind romances went the encounter with Tavario proved to be pointless. She waited fifteen years and finally met the man of her dreams, who turned out to be out of her league. It was the final day of February and work started in the morning. The nerves shot through her at a forceful rate. This job wasn't like any other. It was pure perfection. A few days after her failed nuptial she received a job offer.

Apparently, someone who worked with her in Fortazonio referred her. He didn't say who, but stated, *"You're highly recommended."* Full packages; benefits of all kinds, paid vacations, free room and board, a meal allowance; the list went on and on. Seemed too good to be true, but she had done her research. This was a legit organization with over twenty years of experience. You had to be invited to work for a place like this. They had no interview process.

Golbrosi Enterprise International

The following morning, Tahira woke up extra early for work. It was the first day and she wanted to make a great impression on her boss.

"Welcome to GEI Ms. Zagori, we've been expecting you," the secretary states when she enters the office.

"How do you know my name?"

"It is our business to know the names and faces of all our employees.

Have a seat. Mr. Yarbrough will be with you shortly."

"He's ready," the secretary indicates.

Straightening out her dress Tahira nervously walks into the office. "Good day Mr. Yarbrough."

"Have a seat. Call me Xylon. Relax. You already have the job. Why the perplexed face?"

"I find it strange that you would call and offer me a job based on a recommendation and not even do any type of interview."

Xylon puts down his cup of *Cobalt Tea*. "I know what I want and I trust my informant's judgment. I was told that you love to travel. This is exactly what I need for my Assistant."

"An assistant position?"

"Is that a problem?" he asks.

"On the phone you said I'd be VP of Corporate Development."

"You are. My definition of that. You are my Assistant. My right hand woman. I need someone to join me on my business travels. What countries have you been to?"

"Grand Sierra Isla and Ruvenivi."

"Any country that isn't in Starr Islands?" Xylon probes unimpressed by her previous answer.

"No sir."

"I wonder if I should risk it. I wanted someone who's traveled the world."

"I'm willing to travel sir," Tahira announces nervously. The meeting didn't seem to be going well.

"Xylon," he corrects. "Willingness isn't enough, but I'll take a chance because of your recommendation. Do you accept the position?"

"I'm here aren't I?"

"Great. That is all. The secretary will give you the keys to your condo. You may leave my office."

"O-okay," she responds offended by his insolence.

"And Tahira—"

"Yes?"

"Smile. I'm not going to bite."

Closing the door Tahira breathes a sigh of relief. Her dream was about to come true; traveling the world. This would be the beginning of an epic adventure. What could go wrong?

10

"Good day, Mr. Yarbrough's office, Tahira speaking. On Wednesday? Yes, I will tell him."

"Who was it?"

"That was Mr. Vasconcelos reminding you of your meeting on Wednesday."

"Are your bags packed?" Xylon inquires.

"Why?"

"You're coming with me. I don't travel without my Assistant. These past four months working with you has been blissful. I can see why you were recommended. Tahira, you're the **best**."

"No need for flattery sir, you're my boss. It is my job to make yours easier."

"I don't want easy; I want the job done."

"Where are we going?"

"Sao Paulo," Xylon announces.

"As in ***BRAZIL***?"

"Do you know of another?"

"That's where the meeting is?"

"Yes." Xylon types on his laptop then continues, "Our flight leaves in the morning as we have a connection to make. We're spending two days in New York. I have a meeting there as well. Otherwise, I would've taken the direct flight from Voque to Sao Paulo. You get to see two states and be in two continents in less than a week."

"This is unreal."

"It's real Tahira. Very real. I'm going to show you the world."

JFK International Airport

Terminal 8

Concourse A

"Passengers arriving from Voque on Zonaios flight 218, your bags are located on carousel number 10."

"I got it Tahira."

"Thanks Xylon," she says allowing him to carry her luggage.

A man with a **Yarbrough** placard stands looking extremely stern dressed in all black limousine driver attire.

"That's us. Come on let's go. We'll be stopping for lunch."

"New York eateries, I'm excited."

Xylon places their luggage in the limo trunk.

Inside the vehicle he hands her a glass of sparkling cider. "To a great experience."

"To a great experience," Tahira echoes.

New York. New York. The Big Apple she'd heard people on TV say. The city that never sleeps. She squealed in anticipation as the limo pulled away from the curb. The Borough of Queens was a beautiful sight, with plenty of houses and colors. It was July so the air was scorching. A whopping 95°, but it didn't matter. Anything beat the rainy weather of Voque this time of year. She was in NEW YORK!!

Lunch was excellent. New York with its multicultural cuisine can definitely make a woman put on weight. I've never heard of Trini food before. I love the food in Fortazonio, but that Chicken Roti was indescribable.

11

"Make yourself comfortable," Xylon states when they arrive at the hotel. "My room is next door if you need anything. You're free to roam the hotel, but please don't wander off the premises alone. After my meeting we will go sightseeing."

"Thank you Xylon. This is the **best** job **ever**. You are the **best** boss **ever**."

After getting out of the shower, the piercing sound of the hotel telephone startles Tahira. It was less than two hours since their arrival at the hotel.

I'm not expecting any calls.

"Hello?"

The voice on the other end sounded raspy, like a recording. "Hello Tahira."

"Who is this?"

"***What you did to the Manantes' family has made our leaders VERY angry. You WILL pay…***" The phone clicks off.

In a panic Tahira runs to Xylon's door pounding profusely. "XYLON. XYLON. Open please."

Yawning Xylon opens the door. "Is everything alright? I was taking a nap."

"I'm s-scared s-sir."

"Come in." He watches as Tahira holds her chest in agony. "What's wrong?"

"Someone threatened me," she pants. "They called me on the hotel phone. How'd they know I am here?"

"Who are **they**?"

"I don't know, but they certainly know me and my whereabouts."

"Okay Tahira, calm down. Do you want me to have my team trace the phone call?"

Noting her bosses' concern she stops whining. "I'm sorry, I shouldn't have disturbed you. I know you have your meeting later. I'll go back to my room."

"I'm here if you need me. Let me walk you back."

"It's only a few feet away."

"You're my right hand woman, I can't afford for anything to happen to you. Not on my watch." Xylon grabs his room key.

12

Lights. Camera. Action.

The brightness of the city lights make you think it's daytime. Thousands of tourists were gathered around the many entertainment venues. They'd decided for their last night to dine at *Fiori Toscani;* a premier Italian restaurant.

"Buonanotte, signore e signorina. Posso prendere i tuoi ordini?"

"You can order first," Xylon tells Tahira.

She immediately thought back to her lunch date with Tavario. Italian food. Italian waiters. It was too much.

Xylon glares at Tahira, then turns to the waiter, "Give us a minute sir."

"Why didn't you order?"

"Tahira, what's the matter, aren't you hungry?"

"I'm not ready to date again," she blurts.

"Date?" Xylon scoffs. "Is that what you think this is? Don't flatter yourself. You're my employee. This is strictly professional. Don't go catching feelings."

"I feel so humiliated. Sorry sir."

"Xylon," he corrects.

13

The ride to the airport was extremely awkward. Her assumptions of her boss' niceness had changed the atmosphere.

"Are you going to remain silent for the entire ride?"

"Sir-"

"How many times do I have to correct you, Tahira? I've been correcting you for months. Relax."

"What happened last night will never happen again. I am sorry I assumed you were trying to be more than a boss to me. I've had a rollercoaster of experiences with men for a little over two years and I'm on edge about allowing anyone else in my space."

"I'm not interested in your love life Tahira," Xylon answers with derision. "As I said before, we're strictly professional. I'm a nice person so I will do nice things for you. I don't want to have to fire you because I like you. You're the most competent worker I've had in years. I would like to keep it that way. No hard feelings, but you need to control your emotions."

"It's just the things you say and do sometimes make me wonder, if I'm being honest."

"No need to wonder. You're not my type anyway," Xylon communicates. "You're pretty and all, but I've seen better. I am accustomed to a certain level of femininity."

"What are you trying to imply?"

"If you're going to travel and continue working with me, you need tougher skin," Xylon explains. "I need to know that you are strong enough to endure what the future has. Your trial period is up. Are you ready for the next level?"

"I don't even know what the next level is," Tahira replies.

"**Wrong** answer."

"Is this a game?"

"Do I look like a man who plays games?" he turns his gaze to his laptop. "When you're ready then I'll introduce you to the real work. It will blow your mind."

Real work? What have we been doing all this time?

14

"*Bem-vindo a São Paulo. Temos o prazer de ter você,*" a Brazilian woman asks upon their arrival at the hotel.

Tahira signals to the woman that she doesn't speak Portuguese.

"*Você fala português?*" the woman inquires.

"Xylon help, what is she saying?"

"I'm loving this so much," he teases.

"Do you understand her? You know I don't speak Portuguese."

"Well madam traveler, you have to learn. Where's your translation app?"

"My phone is dead." Tahira shows him her device.

"Portable charger?"

"Buried in my suitcase somewhere."

"Come on Tahira, you're a professional. Start acting like one."

Xylon turns and answers the woman in fluent Portuguese, "*Obrigado pela sua calorosa recepção. É nosso prazer conhecê-lo. Ela não fala portugues.*"

The woman laughs and then responds to the duo. "I speak English a little."

"You can speak English?" Tahira sighs.

"Tahira, she said **a little**," Xylon snaps.

"You want go to your room?" the Brazilian woman inquires.

"How do you say **yes I do** in Portuguese?" Tahira fidgets. "Tell her Xylon."

"*Ela disse sim*," Xylon translates.

"Good, good. I give you dinner."

Tahira stares between Xylon and the woman. "Tell her I am not hungry."

"You will eat. Be kind to our host."

"But, I'm not hungry."

"You will eat," Xylon repeats.

From Voque to New York to Sao Paulo, jetlag made Tahira groggy. The time differences certainly had its toll on her body. They sat down for dinner or *jantar* in Brazil. The night's meal consisted of a bowl of their national dish: *feijoada* and a glass of *caldo de cana*.

"This meal is excellent. Thank you Xylon for introducing me to places I've never been or thought I'd go."

"You're more than welcome. I love experiencing these places through your eyes. Though I've been to Sao Paulo before, it's refreshing to see someone so excited and thankful for the experience. Enough chit chat. It's almost midnight, go sleep. I need you well rested for tomorrow's meeting."

Curiosity hit Tahira. "What meeting?"

"Sleep first and you'll find out tomorrow."

15

"*Indo para a praia?*" the Brazilian woman who Tahira learned was the manager, asks the next morning.

"*Não, temos muito trabalho hoje,*" Xylon retorts.

Tahira stares blankly at the duo. "What are you two saying?"

"Where's your phone?" Xylon mumbles. "I hope you charged it. You need to be a part of the conversation when we meet the client."

"Can you at least translate what was said?"

"She asked if we were going to the beach and I told her we have a lot of work to do," he mumbles impatiently.

"Thank you Xylon for translating."

He points to her phone. "Go on your phone, type in what you just said and say it to me in Portuguese. Let's practice now."

"Is that really necessary? You speak English."

"That wasn't a question."

"Ok sir."

"XY-LON."

"*Obrigado Xylon por traduzir,*" Tahira strains, trying to speak the language.

Xylon claps at her. "*Bom trabalho, Tahira. Mantenha o seu telefone próximo.*"

"Mr. Yarbrough, welcome," an older gentleman greets an hour later.

The man converses with Xylon in Portuguese. Leaving Tahira lost in translation.

"Mr. Vasconcelos, this is the VP I was telling you about, Tahira Zagori."

"Welcome Tahira. I've heard so much about you." The man shakes her hand.

"You speak English. Whew." Tahira replies, thankful for the man's ability to speak a language she understood.

Mr. Vasconcelos glances at Xylon, "I don't understand."

"She's been lost in translation lately," Xylon replies.

Amused at their banter, Mr. Vasconcelos pours glasses of an unknown drink. He hands a glass to Tahira, "Drink."

She puts up her hand in resistance. "What is it?"

"That is rude to ask our host," Xylon tells Tahira, conveying his disappointment.

"What if I'm allergic?"

"Excuse us sir," Xylon grumbles.

Outside of the office Xylon speaks to Tahira in a tone she'd never experienced with him. "What stunt are you trying to pull here? Do you know how important this client is? The man offered you a drink, drink it. You think I would bring you in a harmful environment?"

"I just asked what it was, what's the big deal?"

"You're acting unprofessional Tahira."

"I'm lost, since when is asking a question acting unprofessional?"

"You need to leave." Xylon pulls out his cell. "I'm requesting a **Rapid** to take you back to the hotel."

"Are you serious?"

"Do you want to be a part of this business or not?"

Tahira begins to go into total defense mode. "You're making threats."

"Answer the question. I'm ready to press request."

"I do want to be a part of the business. I'm sorry; I'll keep my questions to a minimum," Tahira hesitantly reassures.

"Great," Xylon smiles. "Now how about those drinks?"

16

Xylon glances over at Tahira. "Are you alright?"

"How long was I out?" Tahira massages her throbbing temples noting that they were in a limo.

He hands her a glass of water. "You passed out."

"That's not what I remember. I missed the entire meeting."

"Mr. Vasconcelos understood. I told him you were jetlagged."

Tahira shakes her head adamantly. "I was fine before."

"It's your body, I have no idea what happened."

"Are you going to tell me what was discussed in the meeting?"

"I'm taking you back to the hotel to rest. We'll discuss it tonight," Xylon replies, dialing a number on his cell.

I don't care what Xylon says, Mr. Vasconcelos put something in my drink. It seems as if he didn't want me to hear what they were saying.

"You look beautiful. Wow," Xylon exclaims when Tahira walks out of her bathroom dressed for dinner.

After the threat in New York he decided to keep a close eye on her.

"Strictly professional remember?" Tahira reminded him.

"Hold on, sorry Tahira you were saying something?"

"Oh, I didn't see you were on a video call."

He closes his laptop. "Ready to go?"

"Who were you talking to?"

"A friend."

"Does that friend have a name?"

"None of your business. Shall we leave?"

"Sorrrryyyy," Tahira drags. "I know you said professional, but I don't know anything about you and it's been months."

"Not much to speak about."

"At least tell me where you're from."

"Why the sudden interest in my life? I'm your boss, that's all you need to know. We're not in the early stages of a relationship so all those typical questions aren't necessary." Xylon opens her front door.

"Whatever. Keep your secrets," she states exiting the room.

"You will pay dearly for what you've done Tahira." The text message came to her phone moments later while in the limo.

"I got another threat." Tahira shows Xylon her cell.

"Are you in some kind of trouble? You're asking me about my background and you're the one who seem to have secrets. Are you a secret agent or something?"

"Agent? Me? I lead a boring life."

"And you're being threatened?"

"Is there a way we can trace these messages? Can you have one of your IT personnel look into it for me?"

"My dear," Xylon scoffs, "your personal life would not be funded by my company. I've already given you enough benefits that would make others jealous. Now you're asking that I WASTE money because you're being pranked? Ignore the messages, when you start getting physical attacks let me know. In the meantime, worry not about **cyber bullies**."

17

"Glória a Deus. Glória a Deus. Aleluia. Deus, você é incrível. Deus você é magnífico. Agradecemos o seu amor, misericórdia, graça, paz..."

The sounds of the cries from Brazilian church next door to the restaurant they were entering for dinner, tugged at Tahira's heart. The atmosphere inside the church resonated through the walls and into the streets. These people meant business. As they cried out to God, it reminded Tahira of the days when her father and the elders prayed. She wondered if they continued in that tradition as she hadn't contacted her family in almost a year.

At the table Xylon observes her facial expression. "What's the matter?"

"Those church people crying out to God."

"I didn't notice. Sounded like noise to me. Thankfully, we cannot hear them in the restaurant," he replies scornfully.

"It's not noise."

"Why so offended? What's it to you? Are you one of them?"

"Them?"

"I believe they're called *Christians*."

"You know what they're called Xylon."

"I'm not religious so I don't care. Are you one of them?"

"I **was**."

"Let's enjoy our meal then," Xylon dismisses. "I'm starved."

When she reaches her hotel room Tahira opens the drawer under the nightstand and finds a Portuguese-English Bible. She picks it up and flips through the pages. Realizing it no longer held the same significance, she puts the book down and heads to the shower.

Glória a Deus. Glória a Deus. Aleluia. Deus, você é incrível. Deus você é magnífico. Agradecemos o seu amor, misericórdia, graça, paz...

That night Tahira tossed and turned. Even though she had no idea what the congregants were saying, she knew that they were crying out to God. It'd been over a year since she went to church or even prayed. These people were strong in their love for God. She somehow knew it. Their prayer played in her mind over and over until she eventually fell asleep.

18

"Hey Tahira, I won't be driving with you to the airport. I have a last minute meeting with a client. Will meet you at the airport. ~Xylon," the text read when she woke up.

Xylon had tried calling her several times that morning, but she refused to answer. The previous night's experience left her drained. She didn't sleep soundly at all. Eventually, she mustered up enough strength to head downstairs for breakfast.

"*Misto quente, salada de frutas, limonada.*" Tahira points out her breakfast choice to the cashier.

Tahira takes out her phone and dials her father's number. After two rings he picks up.

"Hello, daddy."

As her father was about to respond the phone shuts down.

Uggh! I forgot to charge my phone again.

"You finally made it. What took you so long?" Xylon inquires when she arrived at the airport two hours later.

"Why didn't you hire a helicopter for me? The traffic to the airport was terrible."

"I'm sorry; I didn't know you were **my** boss."

"Did you at least check me in?" Tahira asks frantically looking at the departure board.

"You'll have to do that for yourself. Why didn't you Web Check-In? Now hurry, I'm going to the gate, have calls to make."

"Ma'am the flight is cancelled; you'll have to wait for the next flight. I'm sorry," the ticket agent informs Tahira at the counter.

"WHAT?" Tahira panics. "I have a confirmed ticket. No one called me."

"This flight is cancelled," the agent continues calmly.

Tahira pounds the counter. "I'm in no mood for your shenanigans; can I speak to your manager?"

"Oh ma'am, it was my mistake. I typed in the wrong flight number."

Tahira lets out a sigh of relief. "Okay, that I can deal with."

"We have a lot to discuss." Xylon announces when she reaches the departure lounge.

"More travelling?" Tahira replies.

"Yes my love."

"Excuse me, what did you call me?"

Xylon turns his head and shows Tahira his headset mouthing, **I'm on the phone. Shhhh.**

That's strange, I didn't hear the phone ring nor did I see him dial anyone...

19

Thousands of people lined up to watch Tavario Mikos deliver his speech. He was well dressed and stood confident as he spoke to the crowd. Tahira stood next to him as the audience erupts in applause at the sound of her name. He gently squeezes her hand and gives her the mic.

"I don't know what to say," Tahira cries.

"Open your mouth and the words will come," Tavario reassures.

Tahira begins speaking in an unknown tongue. After she spoke many persons came to the front of the stage where she and Tavario stood. He stretches his hands and prays.

The people were crying; some were kneeling on the floor wailing in agony, others rolled. It was a hysterical sight to see if you didn't understand what was happening.

Forty minutes later, Tavario takes a hold of Tahira's hand, leading her off the stage.

"Thank you for walking this journey with me. You are my *Dolcezza* and I love you," Tavario whispers.

Tahira's alarm rang extremely loud the next morning. She didn't notice when she fell asleep. There was something different about this dream.

Why was Tavario still on her mind? She hadn't seen or heard from him since last February.

20

"Happy 25th Birthday to the ***best*** worker any boss could've ever asked for," Xylon announces, with a cake in his hands.

"You didn't have to get me anything." Tahira smiles and blows out the candles.

"I know this will seem far-fetched, but you get me. No one else has ever been able to put up with my ways. What I am trying to say is we **fit**, not in a traditional sense, but what we have is indeed special." He kneels down for added emphasis. "Tahira, will you marry me?"

"I didn't know you viewed me that way. You said *strictly professional*, remember?"

"I know what I said, but I also know what or should I say *who* I want. Tahira, I want you to be my wife."

"I don't even know anything about you or view you in that way. How could I marry you?"

"I had to make sure you were ready for my lifestyle. You've passed all the tests with flying colors." Xylon cuts the cake and hands her a slice.

Tahira stands akimbo. "What tests?"

"All the trips, meetings, conversations… They were all tests. I needed to know if I can trust you. I don't trust anyone else. Trust is imperative in a marriage."

"You don't look like you're kidding."

"When it comes to my life and business I don't **kid**."

"I thought you had a girlfriend. You're always on the phone with someone, although you claim its *business* related."

"If I had a girlfriend I wouldn't be asking you to marry me, now would I?" His voice sounded agitated.

"It's just that—"

"Tahira, I said *no*."

"What about love? Shouldn't you marry for love?"

"We both know that love has nothing to do with our relationship. However, being married wouldn't only catapult me into the big leagues, but you will have unlimited access to money and can travel wherever you want, with or without me."

"As intriguing as it sounds—"

"Think about it. I've only shown you part of the world. With me as your husband the possibilities are endless."

"I'm not sure about this," Tahira groans.

"I said think about it. What do you have to lose?" Xylon insists.

"This is a major step. I'll think about it."

Part Three

1

Tahira stared at the Red Garnet 16K Pave Diamond engagement ring, surprised that she was engaged to a man she didn't love. This situation was unique. Tahira would be able to travel the world using the company's money; **anywhere** she wanted to go, with no strings attached.

It took her two months to agree to his proposal and he had no issue waiting. To anyone looking into her life it'd seem like she settled, but she didn't care. She had no expectations about anything concerning her love life. At least she'd get something appealing out of it, a lifetime of traveling.

"Have you responded to the email I sent you?" Xylon chides when she enters his office.

"Yes, sir," Tahira blurts.

"I'm your fiancé now."

"It'll take getting used to. You haven't even told me where you're from."

"In time," Xylon mumbles, shuffling papers. "Let's keep our focus on work."

"We're engaged and you still don't want to tell me where you're from? What's the big secret?"

"I'm not ready," he retorts.

"When do you want to get married?"

"I'm leaving the wedding details to you. I have more important matters to deal with. I'm changing the location of GEI's headquarters and we'll be moving soon."

Tahira's eyes dart towards the papers on his desk. "Since we're all business, when were you planning on telling me this, **boss**?"

"I'm telling you now."

"I've been down this road before; engaged to a secretive man," Tahira recalls.

"Don't compare me to your ex," Xylon rebukes.

"Am I not allowed to state facts?"

"Go respond to the email I sent you."

"You're dismissing me?"

"Time's wasting. I need your response ASAP. Make sure to fill in the necessary blank spaces." He opens his laptop and begins typing profusely, avoiding eye contact with her.

PRENUPTIAL AGREEMENT

THIS AGREEMENT entered into effective as of the _____ day of
_____, ____.

BETWEEN: **XYLON YARBROUGH** Nionbique, Voque (the 'Future Husband') **and TAHIRA ZAGORI** Nionbique, Voque (the 'Future Wife').

WHEREAS, the parties hereto are contemplating legal marriage; and

WHEREAS, the Future Husband is the owner of the property described above, which is attached hereto and incorporated herein by reference; and

WHEREAS, the parties plan to marry because of a mutual agreement, but the Future Husband does not desire that his current respective financial interests be changed in marriage. NOW, Therefore, it is agreed as follows...

Tahira continued reading the document emailed to her and sighed. Not only wasn't she marrying for love, but her *future husband* wanted a prenup. Knowing the circumstance she agreed to she filled in the date and placed her e-signature on the document.

2

Tahira knocks on Xylon's door. "I'm finished."

"Am I to know what you're referring to?"

"Signing the prenup. Isn't that what you wanted?"

"There, there," he sneers, "no need for that face or body language. Did you think that I'd just allow you to travel free without protecting my assets?"

"I don't know, I've never seen a prenup before," Tahira counters. "Was the **no physical contact** clause necessary? What if we do fall for one another?"

"Prenups can be changed. However, I KNOW my feelings for you won't. Why fix something that isn't broken? You're an excellent employee."

"Whatever."

"Anything else?"

"I was wondering if we could go visit my parents."

"What for?" Xylon insists. "You don't even speak about them."

"I miss them and would like to update them on my life for the past two years."

"Is a face to face visit necessary? Can't you call them on the phone?"

"Xylon, you don't like sharing your life with me, but this is important."

"I don't want to go to Fortazonio."

"You've been there?"

"I know persons who lived there."

"What happened to them?"

"They moved." Noting the perturbed look on her face he continues, "Alright, tell you what; you and your family make arrangements to meet. They can come here or we can go somewhere else. Your choice."

"You'd do that for me?" Tahira gushes.

"Don't be emotional about it. I want you to be mentally solid when we shift gears in our relationship; can't have you breaking down."

Tahira hugs him. "Thanks."

"Don't touch me," he begs, pushing her off.

3

On Friday night Tahira went to the airport to pick up her parents.

"Mom, dad, I'm so excited to see you. Welcome to Voque."

"My child we haven't heard from you in a long time," Ramiro exclaims.

"I needed a break. This is my olive branch to you all. I'm almost 26 and I want us to have a healthy relationship again."

"Why did you invite us here? Why didn't you come back to Fortazonio?" he retorts.

"My husband, be thankful that she reached out to us," Tahiti grins hugging her daughter.

"I have someone to introduce you to," Tahira babbles, escorting them to her car.

"You brought us to another country for an introduction?"

"Dad, let's not start any type of argument. You are still my parents."

"Could've fooled me," Ramiro mutters.

"I'll ignore that," Tahira says. "We're going to meet him at his house. His chef is making us dinner. After that we'll take you to your hotel for the weekend. How does that sound?"

"Haven't seen my child in two years and she has some fancy schmancy new man with his riches," Ramiro chortles, as he enters the car.

SIGH! I hope this weekend isn't a disaster.

"Mr. and Mrs. Zagori welcome to my home," Xylon exclaims opening the door.

"What's your name boy?" Ramiro retorts.

Xylon ushers the family into the living room. "Come in, have a seat. Formal conversation will take place when you're comfortably inside."

"Lovely home young man," Tahiti admires.

"Thank you Mrs. Zagori."

"You can call me Tahiti."

"No honey, let him call you Mrs. Zagori," Ramiro maintains. "Young people these days have no manners; this boy's probably shacking up with my daughter."

"Really dad? No one's shacking up. I have my own place," Tahira placates.

After the initial awkwardness the foursome sits in the living room to converse as they wait for the chef to announce that it was time to eat.

"Are you going to tell me your name?" Ramiro demands looking at his watch.

"Xylon Yarbrough, sir."

"I don't like you," Ramiro blurts. "I'm not going to pretend that I do. What exactly is the purpose of this visit?"

"You don't even know me."

"I'm very good at discerning people. You're hiding something and I don't like to be deceived."

"I have no idea what you're referring to. You can ask me any question you want. I would gladly answer."

"REALLY?" Tahira bellows at Xylon. "You met my dad two seconds ago and he can ask you whatever he wants, but I don't even know where you're from."

"Is this true my daughter?" her father asks.

"What Tahira means to say is—" Xylon begins.

"Don't speak for me," Tahira interjects. "I'm mad at you."

"Give us one second Mr. and Mrs. Zagori." Xylon motions for Tahira to join him outside. "We'll be right back."

"What are you doing?" Xylon rebukes. "This is NOT the behavior you want to display in front of your parents. We must be united."

"How dare you say he can ask **any** question," Tahira snaps, "and all I know is your name."

"Woman, I've told you everything in its time. This is the time for revelations."

"Well **XYLON**, I'd better keep my ears WIDEEEE open."

"Shall we continue?" Xylon suggests when he returns to the living room with Tahira.

"Go ahead Mr. Yarbrough; I'd like to hear what lies come out your mouth," Ramiro murmurs.

"Dad stop, aren't you over your hatred for every man?"

"You're forgetting what you told me about Cadell, I mean Granger?" Ramiro recalls.

"Xylon is not Cadell. You've always taught me to give people a chance to prove themselves."

"I also taught you discernment."

"Please excuse my husband and daughter. They're both strong willed," Tahiti interposes. "I'll start with the first question. Who are your parents?"

Xylon looks down, "I can't answer that."

"Why not?" Tahiti prods.

"Because…"

4

Five minutes later Xylon still hadn't answered Tahiti's question. Instead, his eyes were filled with what looked to Tahira like tears. She'd never seen him cry before.

"Because?" Tahiti edges him on.

"I don't know who they are," he finishes.

Tahira gets up from the chair and stands akimbo. "WHAT?"

Tahiti motions for her daughter to tone down the theatrics. "Let him finish."

Xylon nods with tears welling up. "I'm adopted. I was raised by a couple who I refer to as **aunt** and **uncle**. They took me from an orphanage, raised me, and left this company to me when they passed." He looks at Tahira solemnly, "That's why I didn't want to answer any questions about my past, I don't know it. My aunt and uncle never gave me any details about my origins except that I come from an orphanage. They didn't even tell me the location so that I could've gone and searched for my birth parents," Xylon recounts.

"You're lying young man," Ramiro insinuates. "I can see it in your eyes. That's a horrible story to lie about as thousands of people actually have that kind of life. But, you're not being truthful."

"FATHERRRRR. STOP!!" Tahira fumes. "Why are you trying to ruin my life AGAIN? I know that Cadell was a fraud, but how could you disregard Xylon's life experience? Why would anyone lie about being an orphan?"

"Tahira, what is the purpose of us being here?"

Tahira pauses before answering her father's question. "Xylon is my fiancé and I wanted you all to meet."

"Fiancé? The second man who didn't get my permission."

"He doesn't need your permission, dad. We've agreed to get married and that's that."

"Agreed? Usually in a situation like this the words **we love each other** would be used. Are you marrying a man you don't love?"

"It's my life. I can marry for whatever reason I choose."

"Then why are we here?" Ramiro repeats. "Why did you invite your mother and I if you don't even value our concerns? If you've already made up your mind?"

"I wanted to make amends, but you don't GET IT!!"

"Get what?"

"THAT IT'S MY LIFE," Tahira barks. "Stop being old fashioned and let me live."

"You seemed to be doing fine without us for these past few years. You're the one who contacted us. I am your father and I tell you the truth because I love you."

"But, you don't trust me to make the right decisions for my life," Tahira laments.

While she was accustomed to hearing her husband and daughter's spats, Tahiti recounts her coma and begins to plead with Tahira. "Sweetie, please listen to your father. Didn't you learn from the ordeal with Cadell? I almost died because I didn't follow his leading. Have you forgotten?"

"Mom, things like that happen all the time. You can't say that Cadell and his family was the cause of your coma."

Tahiti gasps. "You're defending that man?"

"I'm not defending him mom. You and dad need to stop. Scary things happened, but there was no proof that any of them made you end up in a coma. Everything else had evidence."

"Wow. Unbelievable," Tahiti cries. "To think I was defending you all this time. Well NO MORE. You're right, it is your life. And you will do whatever you please. As your parents we want the best for you. But, make your choices and live with your consequences. Forget this weekend. We don't need you or Xylon's money; we're going back to Fortazonio. I gave birth to a stubborn daughter."

"Please don't leave when you're angry mom."

"I'm not angry, I'm hurt."

"Tahira," Ramiro interjects, "I'd like a word outside with you before we go."

"You all don't have to leave," Tahira implores.

"It's for the best my child," her father insists.

Ramiro paces the hallway and stops. "I thought after Cadell that you'd take a break and get your life together, but things seem to have gone downhill. When was the last time you prayed or went to church?"

Tahira turns from her father's gaze. "Let's not go down that road. I don't believe in that anymore."

"That's not an answer."

Knowing that the night wasn't going to get any better, Tahira sighs, "It's been a long time."

"I will continue to pray for you. I love you and want the best for not only you, but your legacy."

"What are you getting at?"

"That man, Xylon Yarbrough, isn't only hiding something from you, but he is not your husband."

"You don't even know him. I could understand your reservations about Cadell because you observed him in church and had conversations with him, but this is your first time meeting Xylon. He's a good man. We can grow to love one another."

"Clearly your mind is made up," Ramiro continues. "I won't be supporting or coming to any nuptial you have with Xylon."

"When are you going to release me? You didn't like Cadell. You don't like Xylon. Your issue is that no man is good enough for your daughter. Stop concocting ideas about my fiancé or putting negativity into the atmosphere. When you look for the bad you will always find it."

"I'm not looking for anything negative. I want peace when I give you away to your husband. I haven't felt peace yet."

"YOU need peace? This is **my** life. I'm the one who needs the peace dad."

"Do you have it?"

Tahira shrugs. "It doesn't matter. I've made my choice and I'm sticking with it. Xylon is a good man; he takes care of me, treats me well and supports my likes. What more do I need?"

"You sound like a child," Ramiro counters.

"I don't need any more of your insults. You all could leave. This weekend was a bad idea. At least I tried."

"I know you'll come to your senses one day. Your spiritual eyes will be opened and you will seek after God's will for your life."

"This is the life I chose and if God wants my attention HE'll have to do something **drastic**."

"Be very careful with your words," he reprimands, "you'll remember what you said. I pray that you will experience HIS mercy even in your ignorance."

"Do you want to talk about it?" Xylon queries, when Tahira's parents leave.

"No I don't. I'm going home. We have a busy day at work tomorrow." She picks up her belongings.

"Suit yourself," he shrugs.

5

The weekend went by like a blur. Tahira spent most of her time cooped up in her condo tackling notes for the company.

"You haven't been yourself since your parents left," Xylon notes at the office, four days later.

"Didn't think you noticed," Tahira says, dropping a file on his desk.

"You're not acting like the Tahira I know."

"I have a lot to think about."

"Care to share?"

"Since when do you want to discuss feelings?"

"We're getting married and anything that affects your job performance concerns me."

"Oh wow, it's not even about me *personally*?"

"I didn't mean it that way," Xylon relents.

"Yes you did. I know we're strictly professional. Even in the prenup there are clauses to emphasize that."

"Let's change the subject to something more exciting. Where do you want to go for our honeymoon?"

"What honeymoon?" Tahira groans. "We won't be *doing* anything. Why not stay here? No need to pretend."

"We can have fun like we always do. It's an opportunity to see a new place."

"Well definitely not Mt. Thafivin," Tahira avers.

"Why not?"

"Bad memories," she shudders.

"You never told me you visited there."

"I didn't, but my ex-fiancé is from there," Tahira recalls.

"Alright then, no place that reminds you of him. I don't need to compete with your past."

"Have you ever heard of Agaitimo?"

"Are they a boy band?" Xylon jokes.

"Ha. Those still exist? No it's a…" Tahira pauses when she notices the smug grin on his face. "Never mind."

"Tell me."

"It's fine Xylon. I think we should go to Greece."

"I'll pass. I don't like it over there."

"It's where I really want to go. It'll be a memorial trip on behalf of a friend of mine who died."

"You want us to go on our honeymoon to honor a dead person?" Xylon sneers.

"He was special to me."

Pausing from typing, Xylon drawls out his response, "OH, it's a **he**? That's a definite no. How special was this man to you? He had to mean something. You didn't even want to visit your parents residing in Starr Islands, yet you want to go honor a dead man? I don't like it. We'll talk about that another time."

"Why are you getting defensive? He was my friend."

"Is this dead man the reason you and your ex-fiancé broke up?"

"EXCUSE ME?" Tahira bellows. "Don't bring up my past. We've never had discussions about relationships so don't insinuate anything. You have SOME NERVE."

"I have to ask." He resumes typing. "We've now reached a stage in our agreement where these questions are necessary. In case I may need to add another clause to our prenup."

"What else do you want from me? We're not marrying for love and I can't get anything out of the agreement except free travel."

"Why are you catching an attitude? This is what you agreed to. You can't un-sign the papers," Xylon chuckles nonchalantly.

"I don't want to. Just don't play with my emotions in the process."

"Are we having our first argument?"

"This isn't a joke," she states defensively.

"Whatever, we're heading over to the new location today. The movers will be here shortly. Get yourself together."

Tahira stares at the ring on her finger.

What have I gotten myself into?

6

"You can put that box right there. Leave that photo; I will deal with it myself," Xylon tells one of the movers.

"What exactly do you want me to do?" Tahira wonders, scanning the crowded room.

"Make yourself useful and assist in unpacking the boxes."

"Why are you speaking to me like that?"

"I told you to get yourself together. Deal with your emotions. You seem to be changing ever since you signed the prenup. We're still boss-employee, remember that."

"We're whatever suits *you*," she counters.

"I don't care about your sarcasm. We have lots to do before dinner. I think you should go buy a new outfit. You need to start dressing like my wife."

"What's wrong with how I dress?"

Trying to avoid eye contact with an irate Tahira, Xylon calmly states, "You show too much skin. Can't have my wife exposing her body for the world to see."

Red flags went off in Tahira's head. "If I didn't know any better I'd think—"

"Think what Tahira?"

"Nothing. I had a flashback to a situation I experienced some years ago."

"Do we need to set up some sessions for you to see a Psychiatrist?"

"That won't be necessary. I'm mentally stable."

"I need more than stability. You need to be solid."

Tahira motions towards the doorway. "Can I go now? I want to take a walk."

"Don't go too far," Xylon replies. "I need you to send some emails for me."

"We're so different from when we first started," she sighs.

"What's that you said Tahira? I couldn't hear you."

This man is trippin'…

Tahira returned from her walk and entered her fiancé's office. "Xylon, can I—" Tahira picks up a photo on his desk.

This couple looks like Cyra and Quintos.

"Why are you touching my belongings?" Xylon rebukes.

The sound of Xylon's voice makes Tahira jump and she drops the picture frame.

"Foolish woman. STOP TOUCHING MY THINGS!!"

"You're yelling at me?"

"I apologize. I didn't mean to raise my voice." He bends to pick up the picture. "This picture is important to me, it's the only one I have of my aunt and uncle. I don't want anything to happen to it."

"Maybe you should see a Psychiatrist."

"I'm fine."

"Where was that picture taken?"

Xylon sweeps up the shards of glass. "I don't know. They went on vacation somewhere."

Tahira peers over his shoulders at the photograph. "They look familiar to me."

"I'm sure they do. Everyone in this world has a look-alike."

"That's probably it."

"Ready for dinner?"

"Let me grab my purse."

Taking one look at the picture again, Tahira made a mental note to research Xylon's aunt and uncle. Their resemblance to the Manantes was too uncanny.

"Looks like there's a crazies convention in town," Xylon chuckles, pointing through the restaurant window.

"What do you mean?"

"Those people over there. How they're dressed."

"Reminds me of the members of Agaitimo."

"Your boy band?"

"It's not a band. It was a cult from Mt. Thafivin that got shutdown by the RPF and NIU."

"When did that happen? I'm up-to-date on current events and didn't hear anything like that in the news."

"Seriously?" Tahira exclaims.

"Are you pulling my legs? What's this Agaitimo to you? You keep bringing it up. WAIT was your ex in a cult? Were you in a cult?"

"He was," Tahira sighs, recounting the horrendous experience she had in her early twenties. "I almost joined it without knowing. Long story."

"I'm glad you didn't join. I'd have lost an excellent VP and wife." Xylon places his hand on her hand.

"Was that a compliment Mr. Yarbrough?"

"Don't get any ideas."

They both laugh.

7

Opening the door, Tahira hears a voice that was all too familiar.

"I need someone to help me with this conference."

"Everything will work out Tavario. We will continue to pray that God sends the right person," the woman standing in front of his desk reassures.

"This conference is important. We're going to train men and women to go out and share the Gospel of Jesus Christ," Tavario announces.

"I know, you mention it every chance you get," she continues.

Tavario looks at his laptop. "I'll continue making the calls, there must be one person."

The woman motions towards a nearby chair. "In the meantime I'll go over the names of the applicants for the conference."

Tahira knocks on the door; feeling sorry that she'd listened in on their conversation. What conference was he referring to? How'd she end up where Tavario was?

Entering the room, she reaches out to him, but he pulls his hand away.

"Tavario, it's me Tahira I—" she begins.

Why is he ignoring me? He sees me standing right in front of him.

Taking up a folder, Tavario makes his way out of the room, closing the door behind him.

I know we didn't leave on the best of terms, but why did he walk out on me like that?

"Ms. Zagori, a package came for you," a man in uniform states.

"You can see me?" Tahira murmurs.

"Can you sign the form?" he pleads. "I have other deliveries to make."

"Did you see Mr. Mikos walk out of here?"

"Does he work in this building?" the delivery man shrugs. "Never heard of him."

"He was here a few seconds ago," Tahira replies.

"Can you sign or not, I don't have time for this."

She scribbles her signature quickly on the paper and tears the package open. Inside she sees a keychain resembling the one Cadell had given her on their first date. Behind it was a note.

"*We are everywhere. Watching you. Following you. And you WILL PAY TAHIRA, WITH YOUR LIFE. ~Signed, Congregants of Agaitimo, Mt. Thafivin.*"

The beeping of her phone woke her up out of her dreams. It was 4AM. She had to get help. No one was there to keep her safe. She wondered if she could even trust Xylon.

8

The next day at the office Tahira clicks on the search engine.

"Please speak your command," the computer drones.

"Find Tavario Mikos," she intonates.

"I'm sorry; there is no information about Tavario Mikos on this page," the computer dismisses. "Please speak another command."

"TAVARIO MIKOS, VIAS," Tahira yells.

"Finding information on Vias."

Several articles on Vias appear on the laptop screen.

"NOOOOOOOO, I don't want information on Vias," Tahira laments pounding the desk. "I want information about TAVARIO MIKOS."

"Please speak your command."

"STUPID COMPUTER." Tahira shuts down the laptop and walks out the door.

"Where are you going in such haste?" Xylon stops her abruptly in the hallway.

"What kind of computer system do you have?" Tahira sneers. "I was trying to research something and it gave me the run around."

"We're trying out a new OS that only gives one page search results, do you like it?" He smiles enthusiastically.

"Isn't the internet the place to find out **anything?**" she retorts unamused.

"Only if the information is available." Xylon pulls his phone out of his jacket pocket. "Here, use my phone. I haven't updated it with the latest software yet."

"Are you sure?"

"I have nothing to hide. Go ahead. I'll be back for it after my conference call."

Tahira searches for Tavario, but found nothing about him online. Not even an old article.

This makes no sense. Tavario is a popular movie star. His name is always somewhere. The tabloids love him. I don't understand. Not even one article?

As per post-work day custom, Tahira and Xylon heads to their favorite restaurant.

The waiter observes the duo. "Can I take your order?"

"We'll have two *Winter Salmons*, a large bowl of *Quayap Soup* and two sparkling waters."

"Will that be all, sir?"

"Yes." Xylon hands the waiter the menu.

"Thanks for dinner; I really didn't want to cook tonight," Tahira mumbles, putting her phone on silent.

"When we're married you won't have to cook at all. My chef will do all the cooking."

"But you'll have me, your wife."

"I'm accustomed to eating fine cuisine," Xylon scoffs. "Not interested in you cooking any of that bland food from Fortazonio."

"Are you insulting my country? My cooking that you've never tasted?"

"Stop making things about you Tahira. I grew up being fed by chefs. Besides, we'll be too busy traveling to cook anything."

"I've never heard of a man who didn't want his wife's cooking."

"You haven't met all men. Hold on, someone's calling me."

"Can't it wait? We're having dinner," Tahira condemns.

"The food's not here yet. This is a business call. I'll be back."

"Is everything alright?" Tahira wonders when Xylon returns, infuriated.

He waves his phone in the air. "That's what you used my phone to do?"

"What are you talking about?"

"**TAVARIO MIKOS**," he shouts. "Who is he? You have a boyfriend?"

"You're kidding right? Haven't you heard of him? He's an actor."

"I don't care who he is. Why are you researching another man on my phone?"

"He was a friend of mine. I wanted some updates on what he was doing."

"YOU HAVE A LOT OF MALE FRIENDS," Xylon slams his fist on the table, startling Tahira.

"Why are you yelling? This is a restaurant," she hushes.

"I don't care where we are. Don't EVER let me catch you researching, looking at, or talking to another man unless he's your father or you have my permission. Do you hear me?" Xylon rebukes.

"Your permission isn't needed," Tahira retorts nonchalantly. "I know how to conduct myself. We're not even a real couple. Why do you care?"

"We're getting married. That's as real as it's going to get."

"Your outburst was unnecessary."

"It's necessary. Nowadays people have online affairs. How do I know you're not having one?"

"In order for it to be an affair, we'd have to be in a relationship, Xylon. You've said thousands of times that it's *strictly professional*."

"You're my fiancée and I'd like you to show me respect," he demands.

"Respect is *earned*." She picks up a fork, "Dinner's here, let's eat."

"We'll discuss this later," Xylon hisses.

9

Xylon pulls up to Tahira's condo after dinner. "How long are you going to give me the silent treatment?" He parks the car. "I'm speaking to you."

"Whatever we have going on is exhausting." Tahira unbuckles her seatbelt. "You want me to talk; you don't want me to talk? Which is it? What do you want from my life?"

"Do we need premarital counseling? All this pent up anger you have isn't good for our relationship," he states putting his hand on her shoulders.

Tahira gives him an offensive eye. "Premarital counseling? We're not in a relationship. This is a joke. We have a law binding business contract, that's all. No need for counselors. You think this is funny?"

"We leave for our meeting tomorrow. I need you to be mentally ok to deal with the clients."

"Yeah right. Last time I **met** your client, I ended up passed out, DRUGGED," Tahira reminisces. "But you deny it."

"I have no idea what you're talking about. This meeting is serious; you need to be good for the trip. I can't afford for you to have any outbursts on the aircraft."

"I'll be fine Xylon."

"Oh, by the way, the caterer called," Xylon continues after a few minutes of silence. "Please let me know what you want for our reception menu."

"This isn't even a valid marriage." Tahira opens the car door. "I don't know why you insist on having a big celebration."

Xylon leans over and closes the door. "It is a valid marriage Tahira. There are many people around the world who get married and it's not for love. The celebration is necessary for my clients. As I've stated before this marriage will enhance my status in the business sector."

"I don't want to have this discussion with you," she replies in an exhausted tone.

"We're going to discuss it. January is a few months away. Why do you even want to get married on your birthday anyway?" Xylon inquires loftily.

"Ever since I was a little girl it's been a dream of mine to get married on my birthday," Tahira explains.

"Don't expect to get birthday **and** anniversary gifts from me."

"Believe me Xylon I have no expectations when it comes to our so called *marriage.*"

"In other news, we have to hire a new secretary. I got a notice yesterday that ours had a family emergency that needed to be dealt with."

"Oh no, I'll miss her," Tahira replies, relieved at the change of topic. "She didn't say much, but got the job done."

"That's what I like for my business, **Doers.**" Xylon nods with burgeoning excitement.

"I will post the job opening when I get upstairs in the condo."

Sitting in her bedroom, Tahira thought about life. Her life and the mess she'd made of it. But, it was too late. She'd made a choice and was going to stick it through to the very end. Life wasn't perfect and she had to make the best of her situation. Xylon didn't love her and she definitely didn't love him, but their arrangement made sense.

She went to the kitchen to make *Settlers Bake* and an *Emerald Smoothie*, remembering the times she and Kaiora spent discussing life and all the drama that came with it. Though it'd been years since she last saw her, she often wondered about her ex-best friend.

10

Two weeks later, Xylon informs Tahira of a big meeting with potential clients for GEI.

Zacienzo International

Cape Regalo, Kalanailani

Terminal 2

"Tahira, is that you?" a woman calls out zealously.

It took her a few seconds to place the voice. "KAIORA?" Tahira gasps. "I haven't seen you in years. How are you?" she says embracing her former best friend.

"I am great." Kaiora glances at Xylon. "Who is this?"

"This is my fiancé Xylon Yarbrough," Tahira declares with false cheerfulness.

"What happened to Cadell?"

"That's a long story."

"I have time before my flight," Kaiora appeals. "Do you have a few minutes?" she inclines, still glancing at Xylon.

"Actually, we have a meeting to go to."

"It's alright Tahira, " Xylon reassures, ignoring their banter. "Catch up with your friend. I'm going to make a call," he remarks dryly.

"Are you sure?"

He motions for her to go have the conversation.

"You hungry? I can get you something to eat," Kaiora prompts.

"It's okay. I ate on the plane," Tahira utters courteously.

"I haven't seen you in almost five years. Where's Cadell?"

"Hopefully still in jail."

"Jail?" Kaiora asks softly.

"Let me tell you the story."

Twenty minutes later, Kaiora stares in bewilderment at Tahira. "Definitely didn't expect that."

Tahira nods agreeably. "I was the most surprised. Such is life. I'm with Xylon now and its okay. What about you? I see bling on your finger. Married? Children?"

"Yes, I am married. I have a son," Kaiora voices with affection.

"You going to keep me in suspense?"

"Not sure if my story is as exciting as yours."

"Tell me girl."

"I am officially Mrs. Kaiora Canzoniere. My husband's name is Amerigio. We have a 1 year old son, Nizelli," Kaiora denotes.

"Congratulations girl," Tahira chimes. "You finally settled down. You look good. Peaceful."

"It wasn't easy reaching this point," Kaiora clears her throat. "Around the age of 23 I was at the lowest point in my life. The partying and dating all these guys got boring for me. I didn't know what else to do. I moved to Kalanailani to take a breather. Unbeknownst to me trouble was lurking, ready to take me out. I was driving and a vehicle swerved from out of nowhere and crashed into my car. As I laid there flipped over unable to get out of the car I began to cry. It'd been a long time since I spoke to God, but I had an urge to cry out to Jesus hoping HE'd listen to me. I was in no place to make any kind of request from HIM. Still I tried.

I didn't make any promises, I simply asked HIM to help me. Have mercy. I said 'If You're real, reveal Yourself to me.' Then I blacked out. When I woke up I heard beeping, I was in a hospital. Someone saw the car and called the ambulance. It was Amerigio driving back to Bible School from the airport. He came to visit me every day for four months, stating that he needed to make sure I was good. It shocked me, of all the men I've dated none of them ever showed any interested in my life. That's why I never committed. They just wanted a trophy girlfriend, no strings attached. I was ashamed to tell you who I was dating. Mainly high profile stars coming in and out of Fortazonio; hence my distrust with celebrities.

I recuperated and Amerigio helped me to readjust. He took me to a Missions Conference believe it or not, and the speaker shared a powerful message. When he was finished he asked if anyone wanted to have an encounter with Jesus and I went to the altar. Didn't know what the encounter was going to be, but I said HE gave me a second chance at life even in my rebelliousness so I wanted that encounter. I was the only one in that entire conference of about fifty persons who went up. Embarrassed, but determined for change. The speaker told me that I'd been searching in all the wrong places for someone who I was already introduced to; the only one who loved me unconditionally, Jesus Christ. Then he said lift my hands and the encounter would happen.

I lifted my hands and my life flashed back to every event that I experienced as a child. The hurt of continuous rejection. When I was ten and my grandmother died, leaving me in the care of the State. I never knew my parents. No one ever told me where I came from, but that day I realized that Jesus was by my side every moment of my life.

And even though I still felt like that fourteen year old girl you met in Vacation Bible School, I was free. I don't know why my foster parents allowed me to go to VBS when they didn't even believe in God, but I am glad they did. I met you. You became my family. You were there when I got my first apartment at sixteen. But more importantly, Jesus was there.

Then I fell on the floor and wept. I had my encounter. Amerigio was finishing up his final year at Bible School ready to go into the Missions field.

Our courtship was brief as he stated he knew from the moment he rescued me that we were destined to be together. He is a Missionary Pastor. Or should I say we're a Missionary family. I'm actually on my way to meet him and our son in Italy."

"Now that's a story. Girl, I am happy you found what you needed. God. True love. A family. A real home. Everything," Tahira concludes. She ignored the slight twinge of envy that her former best friend married for love.

"What about you?" Kaiora inquires. "Are you happy with your life? I didn't see any sparks between you and Xylon."

"It doesn't matter. We have our reasons for marrying and I'm ok with my choice."

"How's *#Enfuego Missions*? I know that was your big goal after graduation."

"Never went. I've been over Christianity and that lifestyle for a few years now," Tahira declares. "That situation with Cadell changed my entire viewpoint."

"Uh oh, sounds like me. I'm not worried about you though. As you told me a long time ago, we all have our rough patches with Jesus," Kaiora speaks with understanding.

"Those were times when I believed," Tahira mumbles.

"You still believe, you're just fighting it," she remarks reassuringly. "Sounds like they're calling my flight number. Here's my contact information. Let's keep in touch."

11

"You ready to go?" Xylon inclines moments after Kaiora went through the gate.

"Yes, that conversation was emotional," Tahira exhales. "I need to unwind at the pool."

"Check-in for Yarbrough party of two. Adjoining rooms," Xylon states at the hotel counter.

"Mr. Yarbrough, we were expecting you an hour ago," the receptionist utters glumly.

"Had a slight stop to make," Xylon notes. "Are the rooms ready?"

"Yes," the man continues. "The bellhop will take your bags up to your rooms. In the meantime, dinner is served."

"Can I change first Xylon?" Tahira implores.

Xylon taps his watch. "Hurry up. We have a lot to discuss tonight."

Inside her room Tahira sighs. The conversation with Kaiora was more than emotional. Of course she knew about her friend's story, but to see how an encounter changed her life was mind boggling.

Washing her face in the sink she hears the sound for a message on her phone come in. Wiping her face she walks to the device.

"We are everywhere. Watching you. Following you. And you WILL PAY TAHIRA, WITH YOUR LIFE. ~Signed, Congregants of Agaitimo, Mt. Thafivin."

Anxiety set in as tears begin to flow. This message was exactly like the one she had in her dream. She had to show Xylon. He needed to help her one way or the other. These threats needed to end, TONIGHT!!

Making her way outside of her room Tahira bumps into a man.

"Sorry sir—"

She didn't get a chance to finish her sentence as blackness shrouds her face.

12

"Remember me?" a voice booms violently, as Tahira's eyes adjusts to the sudden burst of light.

"Mr. Vasconcelos," she gasps. "What are you doing here?"

"Kidnapping you of course," he utters smugly.

"How'd you know where I'd be?" Tahira moans, fidgeting with the handcuffs.

"I am the BOSS of this operation."

"What are you talking about?"

"Agaitimo," Mr. Vasconcelos pauses for emphasis, "my baby. And you were responsible for getting the Leaders and my nephew arrested."

"Of course," Tahira's mind instantly flashes back, "the drink in Sao Paulo. There was something you didn't want me to hear. But, what does Xylon have to do with this?"

"Haven't you figured it out by now?"

"Figure what out?"

"Xylon is a member of Agaitimo," he rants. "Well he's a new *Controller*. After you made the RPF and NIU shut down our operation I had to change the *Missions* strategy. You knew too much and I couldn't make things obvious."

Tahira reflects on the time she'd spent with Xylon, her insides seething as the realization hits. "He's been playing me this entire time? Why didn't I put the pieces together? It makes sense. His behavior. The prenup. That's classic Agaitimo, especially the no *physical contact* part. But, how was he able to make me change my mind? He never pinched me or anything."

Mr. Vasconcelos plays with her hair, ignoring her obvious disdain. "Every time he corrected you and told you to say **Xylon**. I figured, what better tactic of mind control than someone stating their name. It was so simple, yet you didn't figure it out. We also included Xylon speaking to an anonymous person on the phone and randomly paying you compliments then switching up stating that he wasn't speaking to you; all to get you to say yes to his proposal. Simple, yet BRILLIANT."

Tahira fidgets with the cuffs. "Xylon lured me here to get kidnapped?"

"Precisely. Now you WILL get married and you will be brainwashed and become a *loving devoted beautiful subject*," Mr. Vasconcelos divulges.

"Over my dead body."

"Now, now, let's not call death upon your life. We need you. I am sure with some minor adjustments we can change you to suit our standards."

"Does Xylon know where you're taking me?"

"He knows everything. He's meeting us at the conference. That's where I'm taking you. We're going to make a public spectacle of you in front of **all** the Congregants. Then we're going to perform the marriage ceremony and whisk you away to our new HQ where you'll undergo the **deactivation** process."

"You're not going to get away with this Mr. Vasconcelos."

"This isn't the movies Tahira. This is real life. It all ends here. When you're deactivated you'll have no recollection of your life before."

God, I know that I don't even deserve to ask YOU for anything, but please SPARE MY LIFE…

13

Xylon walks with Mr. Vasconcelos to Tahira's prison. "Do you have the *subject?*"

"Yes Xylon," Mr. Vasconcelos retorts abruptly. "Now let's get on with this stupid ceremony so we can continue with the conference. We're going to take over the world."

When they enter the room, they note Tahira twitching.

Mr. Vasconcelos shakes his index finger at her. "Uh, uh. No escaping this. You've created enough trouble for me and my organization," he snorts.

She looks at Xylon, "You lied to me." Spitting on him, Tahira starts to run out of the room.

Clenching his jaw Mr. Vasconcelos barks at Xylon, "GET HER."

"Get off of me Xylon," Tahira insists. "I don't want to marry you or join Agaitimo. How could you do this to me? I trusted you."

"I only wanted to follow his orders," Xylon whispers.

"Whose orders? Your LEADER?"

"Vassos."

"Pay attention to everything that's about to happen," Xylon whispers, removing the handcuffs from Tahira. He pulls her on to the stage.

"Ladies and gentlemen. Members of Agaitimo. Congregants from near and far. We are gathered here to witness the GREATEST union of a *Controller* and *subject* in the history of our organization. The union of Xylon Yarbrough and the *subject* we all HATE, Tahira Zagori," Mr. Vasconcelos' voice travels across the audience. The congregants boo at the sound of Tahira's name. He looks around, "Now, where is my officiant?"

Out strolls Olympia with the world's haughtiest grin. Tahira stares in dismay at the woman she thought was her friend. They were ALL members of Agaitimo. She was set up from the very beginning. Was Tavario a member as well?

"We are gathered here to witness history in the making," Olympia imparts, "an untelevised event that would be told for generations to come. Today is **DECIMATION**; the taking down of an empire that killed my fiancé, his sister and anyone else in their path. You all thought that you were gathered here to witness an embarrassment of Ms. Tahira Zagori. Oh no, you're here because you've all been *SET UP* by the Captain of the Ifeto RPF, Mr. Xylon Yarbrough. ***Sandstorm***."

At the sound of the code word, half of the 40,000 member audience pulls out handcuffs, arresting the individuals standing next to them. Each Congregant was standing next to either a RPF Officer or member of the NIU.

DECIMATION was a success.

Mr. Vasconcelos bounds down the stage in an attempt to escape.

Xylon runs after him and slams the handcuffs on his wrists.

"YOU IMBECILES RUINED MY ENTIRE LIFE'S WORK. YOU

HAVEN'T SEEN THE LAST OF ME," Mr. Vasconcelos snarls as another NIU Agent escorts him out of the auditorium.

14

After minutes of disorientation, Tahira walks toward the group of agents. "Olympia, why are you always the one to come out and make these revelations? What is the meaning of all this?"

"You'd want to sit down," Olympia beckons. "I'm sorry girl. We had to. Vassos made me promise that if anything ever happened to him, I'd take care of you."

"He knew he was going to die?" Tahira entreats.

"It's the life we live as agents. We're powerful, but not invincible. We bleed just like everyone else."

"I'm confused."

"Sit down Tahira. You've been through a lot."

"I don't want to sit down Olympia. I want an explanation. At least give me that."

Olympia reveals the full details of the mission to Tahira. "The day after we left you to pick up the pieces of your broken heart from your failed nuptial we received word from Siren, in Sao Paulo at the time, that twenty people were spotted at GRU Airport dressed in Agaitimo like clothing.

She followed the group to Mr. Vasconcelos' office and overheard them discussing a TAKEOVER. Somewhere in the exchange she heard one of the members referring to Mr. Vasconcelos as the **BOSS**, the one in charge of creating Agaitimo. They wanted to set up camps all over the world in the financial hubs; New York, Sao Paulo, you name it. Acting fast she contacted NIU HQ and told me about the takeover.

I contacted our connection in Starr Islands and we began putting together our operation. We needed someone willing to double-cross the Founder of Agaitimo. However, none of the RPF Officers wanted to take on such a huge task. They feared for their family's safety.

Days later we got a call from the Ifeto station that their captain volunteered himself. It was hard to get him in Agaitimo as those who'd fled trusted no one. We set up a fake organization, with a long history of financial success, a backstory for Xylon and e-mailed Mr. Vasconcelos. Xylon had several meetings with him before Mr. Vasconcelos trusted him. He convinced him that he could get you Tahira. This sealed the deal. With the BOSS' approval we now had an in.

Siren gave Xylon your number and he offered you the job of a lifetime. He set everything up, even the prenup. It was all fake; he was never going to marry you. He promised to protect you through the operation. Because of your connection with Agaitimo members before, we used that knowledge to our advantage; knowing that anyone who seemed off the charts, you'd react. Everything had to be convincing.

Siren's been there all along as a backup using prosthetic faces. We needed an NIU agent capable of pulling off something to this magnitude. The day she 'quit' GEI was the day we knew everything was aligned perfectly for **DECIMATION**. In Sao Paulo, she was the hotel manager. You know the Portuguese speaker who spoke *a little English*. In Voque, she was Xylon's secretary hiding in plain sight, not *saying much*. Siren is our most prized agent. A Mistress of Disguise; trained in Cybernetics and Linguistics.

She knows over one hundred languages fluently and has an accelerated brain capacity to pick up any new language in seconds. She's THAT good. Xylon convinced Mr. Vasconcelos to allow her to assist them. Mr. Vasconcelos would message Siren whatever he wanted to say and Siren would **deliver** them to you. No one could trace it back to him. Xylon had to make the promise. It worked and they were able to deliver several messages to you. Every business call that Xylon made was to HQ to keep us up to date. Your father almost blew Xylon's cover when he stated that Xylon was hiding something. Thankfully, you dismissed him or the operation would've been a bust. We could use a man with your father's intuition on our team.

We never meant for it to get this far, but time ran out and we had to act fast when Mr. Vasconcelos decided to change the date of the conference. I did all this for Vassos and Zerenia. I hope you're not upset Tahira," Olympia finishes.

"How do you know it's over? That all the Congregants were captured?" Tahira inquires, without skipping a beat.

"Members of Agaitimo are loyal to their Leaders. We had to trust their loyalty. Xylon was responsible for this leg of the operation. He suggested to Mr. Vasconcelos to have a **Conference of Humiliation** where all the Congregants would see firsthand the person who got their Leaders arrested. It was historical so everyone wanted to be there."

"And you're sure you got ALL members of Agaitimo from around the world? What if there's more?"

"We're always on the lookout," Olympia claims, "but that isn't for you to worry about. Go live your life in peace. You can't run forever. Xylon told me you were a Christian. I'm sure the God you served will have mercy and protect you. Have a great life. Hope you come to visit us in Greece one day."

Tahira turns to her now fake ex-fiancé, "Xylon, thank you for protecting me. I wasn't sure about you, but I'm glad that I stuck through it for my own sake and safety."

"Sorry I had to be harsh with you at times," Xylon apologizes. "I knew it was important for me to take this operation seriously. Everything had to look real."

"I understand. I'm just glad you didn't pinch me."

The two laugh.

"Go Tahira. You are now free," Olympia urges.

15

Port of Eights, St. Jannaio

A year had passed since the entire ordeal transpired with Tahira and the members of Agaitimo. In two months she'd be turning 27 and life was good. After the agents left her to pick up her life, yet again, she took time off to recuperate and rededicate her life to Christ.

After the time of consecration, the Holy Spirit urged her to contact the Director of *#Enfuego Missions,* Mrs. Sunday Noiyin and she agreed to go through their rigorous training process. Knowing all that happened in the first half of her twenties Tahira was ready to live a peaceful life sold out to Jesus. No man. No drama.

St. Jannaio was a quiet and serene oasis for a Missionary. But, it wasn't all relaxation as there was work that needed to be done. Many souls were saved through the work that *#Enfuego Missions* did. They had programs to help people no matter their status in life.

Tahira's heart gravitated to the orphanage. She wasn't sure if she'd get the opportunity to become a mother, but these children brought joy to her heart. The members of the team were focused on the task at hand. Not one of the single men in the group tried to hit on her, though she was sure they noticed her.

Outside in the Orphanage Courtyard, one of the toddlers begins to wail.

Tahira rushes, scoops up the baby girl and sings to her. Immediately the infant places her head on Tahira's shoulders, falling asleep.

"I like this look for you," Sunday admits. "You'll make an excellent wife and mother someday."

"I've been here a year and none of the men have even blinked in my direction."

"They're not the ones for you. Who said you had to meet your husband in St. Jannaio? I have a feeling you'll meet him soon though."

"**Soon?** Such a vague time. Thank you Mrs. Noiyin, but my mind isn't on marriage or children. I enjoy working in the Orphanage. These babies are my children."

"Yes, but you're only 26 years old. God has much in store for you. You will get married and have children one day."

"I used to think that, but after two failed engagements I highly doubt that's in the pipelines for me. I'm good with Missionary work."

"Admirable, but it's not meant for you to do alone. Even the disciples went out in twos," Sunday chuckles.

Tahira giggles, "Great analogy."

"Oh," Sunday stops, "before I forget, there's a camera crew coming in to do a short video on the Orphanage. We're sending it to all the Churches in Starr Islands to encourage other young people to join #EnfuegoMissions."

Tahira grimaces. "I don't like cameras, but I will help in any other way that I can."

"All you have to do is be yourself. Ignore the crew and act natural. It's not a movie."

"Movie or not; I like the background," Tahira stresses.

"Sorry to burst your bubble, but being a Missionary will put you in the foreground, a lot. You'll do well. Maybe a man may see you on TV and fall in love," Sunday croons.

"I highly doubt that. I'm going to grab a late breakfast. See you later."

16

An hour later, the orphanage resembled a movie set. Tahira fidgeted apprehensively as the camera lights turned towards her.

"We're live here today at *St. Jannaio Casa Dell'Eredità*. Joining is Missionary Tahira Zagori. Tahira, can you tell us what you all do here at the Orphanage?" The interviewer places the mic in front of her.

"Sure," Tahira exhales. "Monday through Friday the students, as we like to call them, go to school at our school house. We start with a morning chapel service with worship and devotions, followed by a biblically based school day, learning each subject through the lens of the Bible. We provide them with three healthy meals daily, uniforms, and everything else they need to have a proper education."

"That sounds awesome. What else can you tell us?"

"Our Orphanage is paired with the **Royal Adoption Agency** in Kalanailani, and together we work toward having each student adopted by a family from any country in the world. Students are sent here by various agencies that have trouble finding homes for the children. We currently have two hundred children ranging from 8 months to 14 years old. No child stays in the Orphanage for more than a year as we prayerfully find the right families for them."

"That sounds amazing," the interviewer retorts impressed. "How do you fund this Orphanage? How are teachers and other workers paid?"

"Everyone who works here came in as a volunteer. No one receives a salary. But, every worker comes from a specialized field that aids in the teaching of our students. Our funding comes from Churches, Bible Universities, HRH King Hezion and various sectors of Starr Islands."

"Can you tell us about the Founder?" his eyes glance at Sunday.

Tahira looks nervously at Sunday who motions for her to answer the question.

"Our organization was started in 2004 by Mrs. Sunday Noiyin - a native of St. Jannaio - at the age of 16, after she went to a meeting at the Palace between students and members of the world's largest adoption agencies. They were aiming to develop a program where orphans usually not chosen could be adopted. She was selected as the student representative and given five months to develop a plan for this program. Being an orphan at one time herself, she knew exactly what they needed. And the rest is history."

"Thank you Ms. Zagori," he motions for the cameraman to change direction. "As we continue our interview, let's meet some of the students…"

"How'd I do?" Tahira stares at Sunday awaiting the critique.

"Tahira, you were wonderful. I am proud of you. You were able to capture the essence of this Orphanage in less than five minutes. But, more importantly you were relaxed and relatable. I'm glad that you faced your fear head on."

"Anything to help you."

"I'm going to speak to the crew and then its lunchtime. Don't forget our end of year celebration is at 2PM. I can't wait to see what your students put together."

On December 3rd, Sunday drove Tahira to the airport. As the only member of staff who lived away from her family, Tahira was granted a one month leave to spend with her family. During this month she would prayerfully decide if she wanted to stay on with *#EnfuegoMissions* for another term.

Sunday hugs Tahira. "Enjoy your time off with your family. You definitely deserve it. You've worked so hard this year."

"I'm going to miss my babies," Tahira cries.

"You'll see them soon." Sunday waves to her as she enters the airport.

17

Tahira arrives at her parents' house at 7:30 that night; eager to see her family and have a long overdue reunion.

"My daughter you are back," Tahiti sniffles. "Those video calls weren't enough. There's nothing like seeing my baby girl face to face. Where I can hug and squeeze her."

"Mom, I'm hardly a baby." Tahira squirms at her mother's tight embrace.

"You'll always be my baby."

"Where's dad?"

"Prayer meeting. Where else do you think he'd be?"

"I'm glad to see that they've kept it up."

"After everything that happened between our family and the Manantes', Pastor Hizaor decided to emphasize the importance of prayer. We now have All Nights for the Women and Youths as well. You've also inspired us to get back to Missions. We're starting as early as next year; with plans to send teams out to various countries in Starr Islands, then eventually the world," Tahiti discloses.

"This is amazing. Glad that I am a pioneer of sorts."

"With that being said, we got to get you married off. You can't stay single forever."

"No thanks mom. I don't need your help."

"Don't worry. I have no *potentials* for you."

"Whew," Tahira chuckles. "We see what happened the last time."

"Years ago. Old news. You just missed Kaiora and her family. Lovely family she has."

"I'm planning on seeing her before I return to *Port of Eights*."

"Awwww that's good," her mother rejoices. "She was a great friend to you. I'm glad you all made up."

"Me too mom. Now with all of that said, what did you cook?" Tahira begins to sniff the air. "I'm starving."

"Food's in the oven. I'm going to go finish up preparations for the Women's Yearend Gala tomorrow night. I bought you a dress, you can wear that. Real pretty. Take some pictures maybe post it online. Some fella's bound to see you."

"MOM!!"

"Just saying, you should always be prepared," her mother jokes.

The following night when Tahira arrives at the gala, she is greeted by the pastor's wife.

"Oh look at you, as pretty as the day you were born," Mrs. Ankara Hizaor beams.

"Minister Hizaor," Tahira grins hugging the woman.

"How are you my darling?"

"I am great."

"I see your ring finger is still bare," she comments. "Your mother told us you're single."

"I'm fine. Nothing's wrong with being single."

"That's right. But a pretty girl like you shouldn't be single forever. Don't worry we have your name on the **TOP** of our prayer list," Ankara announces.

"Embarrassing," Tahira cringes.

Everyone's always trying to marry me off. When God's ready my husband will come. Even if I never marry, I am happy with what I am doing for God's Kingdom.

The night's event was filled with questions on Tahira's marital status. She exhaled contently when they arrived home.

Holding the items behind her back, she knocks on her father's study.

"Daddy, can you hold these for me?"

"What is it?" Ramiro inclines.

"Some things I received from an old friend. I don't want to keep it anymore, but I don't feel a release to get rid of them yet."

"Maybe you should sell them," he advises.

"No, they're special. If I ever see the person again, I'll give them back to him. Too many reminders having them in my possession."

"Okay Tahira," her father agrees. "I will keep them in a safe place."

"Thanks dad. Good night."

"Good night sweetie," he replies, returning to his book.

18

"The time went by so fast," Kaiora notes at the end of Tahira's vacation. "When am I going to see you again?"

"We have to plan something."

A boy runs up and taps Tahira, "Aunty Tahira, look what my daddy gave me."

"That's nice Nizelli," she nods to her nephew, "now be careful."

Nizelli laughs and runs out of the room.

Kaiora smiles faintly. "That boy is too much. He's been playing with that toy nonstop. His father spoils him."

"He's going to make a fine husband to a special young lady someday. You all have trained him well."

"Please don't rush my baby's age."

Tahira chuckles. "Girl, you need a mini you. All that testosterone in the house must be exhausting. Nizelli and Amerigio are twins."

"Well…" Kaiora begins.

"Well what?"

"I'm pregnant," she beams nervously.

"Are you serious right now?" Tahira screams in excitement. "How many months? A girl?"

"Four months and yes I'm getting my mini me."

"I'm so happy for you."

"Don't worry girl, your time will come," Kaiora replies thoughtfully.

"What do you mean?"

"Marriage. Family. I know you've had a rough time, but it'll happen."

"I'm fine."

"Pulese," Kaiora rolls her eyes. "Who do you think you're fooling? I'm your best friend, remember?"

"Yeah, I know," Tahira laughs.

"And I know when something's heavy on your mind. What is it?"

"I still love him."

"Cadell?"

"NO WAY," Tahira writhes. "I'm speaking about Tavario."

"A few years ago I would've shut that thought alllllllllll the way down, but you met him and spent time with him already. Anything's possible girl. We'll pray that God will send your husband for you. If it's not Tavario, whoever he is will be better. I know how important it is that your husband *IS* a Missionary, so remember that. You'll get your Missionary husband and be married to the man that God has for you. Don't let your heart be troubled and don't be sad. You're doing what you love; working in God's Kingdom and God knows when it's your time."

"Thanks. Okay enough tears." Tahira blows her nose. "Have you come up with a name for your daughter?"

"We still have time. I'm trying to think of a name that combines three of our names. You know I love unusual combos. If you think of anything though, please let me know."

"Will do girlie. I'd better leave now if I want to catch my flight in the morning."

"Love you Tahira. We'll video call as per usual."

"Yes and I love you too."

19

Five days into the New Year, Tahira returns to St. Jannaio ready to start a new term. She decided that *#EnfuegoMissions* was a part of her calling and she'd stay as long as the Lord saw fit.

"Sunday, I'm back," Tahira announces entering the office.

Sunday motions for Tahira to sit as she was on a phone call.

"Oh sorry," Tahira whispers taking a seat.

Hanging up the phone she speaks, "How was your vacation? How's the family?"

"My vacation was peaceful and relaxing mixed with a little **extraness**," Tahira chuckles. "Family's great. However, the ladies in Church are relentless in trying to marry me off."

"We are all trying to marry you off," Sunday nods.

"How was your vacation?"

"My husband and I got some much needed **us** time on a cruise."

"I'd love to go on one someday. What about the twins?"

"Their grandparents insisted that we send them over for the vacation time. Thankfully, my parents and in-laws live on the same street. So they shared the time. It was perfect. Believe me my husband and I were happy."

"Yes, your children are energetic to say the least. Are they around?" Tahira peers out the window.

"Somewhere in the Courtyard playing with their friends." Sunday's tone changes, "I have some news for you."

Tahira inclines her ear towards Sunday. "I'm listening."

"I just got off the phone with a secretary for a Missions Director based in *Saheluna,* Lux Point Milano. He's been calling around several agencies looking for a volunteer to assist him in conducting a Missions Conference."

"Did they find someone?"

"No, but I volunteered you."

"My class starts back tomorrow," Tahira declines.

"That's not for you to worry about. One of the other teachers can take over while you're away. Besides, this will be good for you. Give you an opportunity to train with a seasoned Missions Director and also break you out of your fear of being in the foreground. You've been on my mind a lot and I've been praying for you to branch out. I know you love the Orphanage, but I don't want you to be comfortable here. There's so much for you to do and I think this is a great start."

"When do I leave?"

"Tonight," Sunday announces.

Saheluna, Lux Point Milano

Tahira makes her way to the taxi driver with a **Zagori** placard.

"I'm Ms. Tahira Zagori. Going to the *Saheluna Royal Hotel.*"

"Right this way miss," the driver takes her luggage and places it in the trunk.

"Can you tell me who I'm meeting?"

"I was only told to bring you to the hotel. I have no further information to give you."

Tahira looks out the car window and sighs. Whoever it was she hoped he was nice.

"We're here," the driver announces.

Tahira proceeds to tip the driver.

"That's okay miss, it's already covered. Go to the receptionist and she will give you further instructions. Have a great night."

Tahira stands stunned as he walks away.

"Name please?" the receptionist asks when Tahira puts her bags down.

"Tahira Zagori."

"Who are you here to see?"

"I was told I'm meeting a Missions Director for a conference. No one gave me a name," Tahira responds in a friendly fashion.

The woman looks up from her computer. "Oh yes, Tahira. You were the woman Mrs. Noiyin told me about on the phone this morning. My name's Cypress, I'm the secretary. The Director hasn't been in for the day, but he should be here shortly."

"He doesn't know I'm coming?"

"He left me in charge of making calls to the agencies to find someone. I haven't gotten a hold of him for the day. Busy man."

"Can you tell me his name?"

"Oh there he is; you can introduce yourselves," Cypress nods at the man entering the building.

The man stares in astonishment. "Tahira?"

Spinning around she gapes in shock at the man standing in front of her. "T-Tavario?"

"What are you doing here?" he replies coolly.

"I came to meet the Missions Director for a conference. Do you know where I can find him?"

"You're looking at him," Tavario beams excited to see her.

"Y-you're the Director?"

"I am. I take it you're the one they sent. What a pleasant surprise."

20

"I don't understand," Tahira mumbles. "What are you doing here in Lux Point Milano?"

He is still the definition of FINATION.

"Missions," he publicizes.

"I haven't seen or heard from you in years. There's nothing about you on the internet. What happened?"

"Let's go over there and talk." Tavario leads her to a nearby bench.

"You look beautiful by the way," he compliments with a reddened face.

"Tavario, focus," Tahira brushes him off.

"Never could take a compliment," he croons.

"Your story?"

He stops himself from looking at her. Her beauty caught him off-guard. "After I left Ruvenivi I finally told my family what happened with me. I'd had a dream and didn't know what it meant, but someone explained it to me. My contract was soon over and I tied up all my loose ends in *Kian-Jion Delta,* Vias. I went to Church with my parents and a Missionary Director came looking for volunteers to enter a training program. I felt a tug at my heart to sign up. This program was for four months. We learned about the Bible and the Great Commission and our purpose as Christians.

I'd always believed in Jesus, but didn't have a relationship with him. The program facilitated the atmosphere for it to take place and I got baptized. I would never forget when we did a 3-Day prayer and fast, my life changed completely. I knew for sure that this is what I was destined to do. So many years I lived my life in the limelight **entertaining** people. With Missions I could show people hope. Hope for a better life. I couldn't have done that as an actor.

I asked my Publicist to remove all content of me from the internet. It wasn't easy and I'm sure there is still information available, but it's so far down on the search pages. People usually only scroll through the first two pages on the search engines for any topic they want.

When training was over I was sent here in *Saheluna* to work with the then Director, who retired last year. I've been conducting training ever since. I also travel around the world to do the same thing."

"This is crazy. It has to be a dream. Pinch me."

"No dream Tahira. Why would I pinch you?"

"Okay, wow. Now that you've clarified your life for the past almost four years, let's talk about the conference. I'm nervous and excited at the same time."

"Why are you nervous?"

"Speaking in front of people has never been my strong point."

"You'll do fine," Tavario reassures. "The fact that you're here means that you're capable. What about you? What have you been up to?"

"HA!! You wouldn't believe me if I told you."

"Try me."

21

Tavario spent the next two days training Tahira and teaching her about missionary conferences.

"Are you ready for the conference tomorrow?"

"Tavario, I don't think two days was enough preparation."

"Everything is already planned. Don't look so nervous. We'll pray and God will have HIS way. This is HIS business, it will go well."

"Easy for you to say, you've been in front of people your entire life."

"Yeah, acting like **another** person. It's not so easy when you have to be yourself. People can hate a character on TV, but when it's you the real person, it's tough," he confesses.

"I've always been a background girl," Tahira signals.

"Either you want to do it or you don't. No one's forcing you. If you want to leave you can. But, I'd really like you to stay."

"I don't want to miss this opportunity. I'll stay. Can you give me some time tonight? To pray and prepare some more?"

"Of course; I wouldn't stop you. Do what you have to. Let's pray before you go to your room," he takes her hands and they pray.

The next morning Tahira stares tensely as thousands of people lined up to watch Tavario Mikos deliver his speech. He was well dressed and stood confident as he spoke to the crowd. Tahira stood next to him as the audience erupts in applause at the sound of her name. He gently squeezes her hand and gives her the mic.

"I don't know what to say," Tahira confesses.

"Open your mouth and the words will come," he replies reassuringly.

"Tahira, you did excellent. When did you learn Greek?" Tavario beams, hugging her before pulling away.

"I've never learned the language; just a few phrases from a friend of mine who passed."

"Well you didn't know this before - so I know it is God who led you — but, everyone in that audience come from Greece. And what you saw taking place was the breaking of bondage for some of them. If you only knew their stories you'd be in awe—" he pauses. "Why are you crying?"

"That wasn't just a freedom story. This happened already for me in a dream I had two years ago, exactly like it did today."

"Was I in the dream?" Tavario beseeches, his countenance shifting to that of solemnity.

The atmosphere had suddenly changed and they both felt it.

"Exactly like it was," she repeats. "I found it strange because I didn't know what you were up to, nor had I heard or seen anything about you. I wondered why you were in the dream, but never got an answer, until today."

His face lights up. "You're her then."

"Who?"

"The woman whose face I couldn't see in my dream."

"I don't understand."

"The dream I had that I couldn't share with you, it was about me being in an audience and a woman standing next to me. Everything that took place today also happened. I just couldn't see her face or hear what she was saying. But, I saw her. I knew that woman was my wife," Tavario proclaims.

All of a sudden her head begins to spin. "Come again?"

"You Tahira, you're my wife. I knew from around the time when I was training, but asked for confirmation. I didn't get it until I saw you on TV."

"When did you see me on TV?"

"You did an interview for *St. Jannaio Casa Dell'Eredità* last year?"

"Yes," she nods.

"I saw it. I wanted to contact you, but the Holy Spirit told me not to contact you and that God will work everything out. My secretary began corresponding with Mrs. Noiyin since the video was released. I didn't know you were a part of her team. Now you're here helping me. This is unbelievable," he boldly confesses.

Not wanting to go through another failed experience, Tahira looks at him for clarity. "Please don't make me cry Tavario. This is happening? Am I dreaming?"

"This is reality. Not a dream. Not a movie. It's happening."

22

Four Months Later

Sunday enters the dining hall and sits next to Tahira. "How has the long distance courting been?"

"I miss him," Tahira blushes. "I really want to introduce him to my parents before we go any further. He's already talking about marriage. We have a date set and everything."

"Long distance relationships are usually hard. When are you all planning on getting married?"

"My 28th birthday. You and your family are invited of course."

"A January wedding. At least it's not winter time in Starr Islands. I await my official invitation."

"I'm going to miss the Orphanage."

"We're not going anywhere, but you need to be a helpmeet to your husband. I am happy for you," Sunday squeals.

"It's really happening."

Sunday squeezes Tahira's hand in agreement. "In God's time and it's *beautiful*. Now go call him. Whenever you're ready to go *meet the parents* with him let me know so I can schedule a substitute for your class."

"*My Dolcezza* I miss seeing your beautiful face in person."

"We have to talk, Tavario."

"Uh oh. I don't like the sound of that."

"Oh, no, no, no," she stops his train of thought. "Hello, I've waited almost twenty years to be with you. You'd really think this is a breakup call? Not even in the movies."

"You almost had me there," he exhales. "I was about to get on a plane to come meet you begging on my knees, *baby please don't leave me.*"

"I see you're still dramatic."

"Always," he jokes. "What did you want to speak about?"

"Before we continue any further in our relationship, I'd like us to go see my parents so we can let them know what's happening. That we plan on marrying soon. I want to do things the right way. Officially introduce you to the Zagori's."

"When do you want to go?" he replies unbothered by her request, a change from her previous *relationship.*

"May is good."

"You do know that's next week right?"

"Yes I know. Why are you smiling? Shouldn't you be nervous about meeting my parents?"

"Good night *My Dolcezza.* See you soon."

Am I missing something?

23

"We're here," Tahira declares, one week later.

"Come in you two," Ramiro greets.

"Where's mom?"

"She's in the kitchen finishing up dinner."

"I'll wait until she comes out to do this introduction."

When her mother joins them in the living room, Tahira excitedly presents Tavario to her parents. "I'd like to officially introduce you both to Mr. Tavario Mikos, my soon to be husband."

"Whoa slow down Tahira," Ramiro teases.

"Tavario, meet my parents Ramiro and Tahiti Zagori."

Her father extends his hand jokingly, "Nice to meet you again son."

Ramiro and Tavario laughs.

"She doesn't know?" Tahiti chimes.

"Know what mom?"

"Tavario has already introduced himself to us," her mother reveals.

"What are you talking about?" Tahira looks at him. "Tavario?"

He takes her hand. "I knew how important it was for you to have your parents' blessing and that you wanted to do things the right way. Before I asked you to start courting I contacted your parents and we set up a meeting right here in Fortazonio. I told your father my intentions and all that good stuff and now we're here."

"Dad, why didn't you tell me?"

"And ruin this moment?" Ramiro laughs. "The look on your face is priceless. This is what I was praying for all along; a man who respected me as your father enough to ask my permission to court you. I know that it's old fashioned, but this was the only way I know how. I did it with your mom and all the men in my family did it with their wives. Tradition is high on my list, but nothing beats respect. This young man has it."

"You approve of him?" Tahira exhales. "Uggh!! FINALLY."

"I have the drinks for toasting and then we eat," Tahiti informs the trio.

"I'm still in shock. You all knew about this? Tavario, you could've said something."

"I always want to surprise you. Keep the spice in our relationship," he winks.

Tahira blushes.

"To Tahira and Tavario. May you have a healthy, long life and marriage fulfilling God's purpose. I love you both. Welcome to the family, son," Ramiro cheers.

"Good night Mr. and Mrs. Zagori," Tavario waves.

"Good night Tavario," Tahira's parents reply in unison.

"I'll walk you out babes," Tahira states closing the door behind them.

"Don't cry," he wipes her cheeks, "you'll see me in the morning."

"I can't wait for the day we don't have to say goodbye anymore," she sighs.

24

"Breakfast time," Tahiti calls.

"*Blossomed Eggs* and *Plumberry Pancakes*," Tahira squeals grabbing a plate.

"They don't feed you in St. Jannaio?"

"There's no cooking that compares to my momma's," she explains mid chew.

"You flatter me. My baby girl is all grown up. About to be a married woman. Soon there'll be grandchildren."

"Let me at least walk down the aisle first."

"I've waited for this day longer than you have. I'm going to enjoy planning a real wedding since I didn't get the opportunity the first two times."

Tahira squeezes her mother's hand. "I'm glad that you're around mom. I wouldn't want to share this experience with anyone else. I love you."

"I love you too my daughter. Don't make momma cry. Mess up this flawless face."

"Haha. You're too much," Tahira grins.

"Sweetie you look beautiful; your first movie premiere. You will be the star of the night."

"I find it strange," Tahira confides in her mother. "Tavario hasn't done anything limelight worthy in years and now he invites me to a movie premiere?"

"Even though he's no longer an actor, it doesn't mean he can't support his friends and their work or attend events."

"I guess you're right. I am really nervous. What if I end up in some kind of tabloid or bad publicity photo?"

"You'll be with Tavario," Tahiti reassures. "Enjoy the time with him. Besides it's an independent low-key film that was made here in Fortazonio. He said it's an intimate gathering."

"Do I look okay?"

"You look beautiful honey. Breathe. Just think about you and Tavario."

"Tavario, Tavario, who is this?" Paparazzi's shout when they arrive on the red carpet.

The flash of the camera lights irritated Tahira, but she choose to smile through it all in support of Tavario and his friends.

"Will you return to the big screen soon?" a cameraman calls out.

"No comment." Tavario gently takes Tahira's hand as they walk in the already dark theatre. She couldn't see anyone.

Making their way to the front of the theatre, Tavario motions for Tahira to sit down. "I'll be right back *Dolcezza*. Don't move."

"Where are you going? The movie's about to start."

"I'll be back," he repeats.

Tavario hadn't returned yet, but she decided to remain seated. Giant letters flashed across the screen.

And Now Our Feature Presentation

THE ROAD THAT LED TO LOVE

This movie surpassed all other movies she'd seen. Including those she saw with Tavario in it. Though it had all the cinematic content and excellent scenes, it was the most creative way anyone could ever propose to her. She began to cry when it dawned on her that it was indeed her **engagement night.**

When she finished wiping her eyes the lights came on and Tavario was on his knees with a ring in his hand. He motioned for her to stand and proceeded with his declaration of love.

"Tahira, the road that led us here, to love, hasn't been an easy one. I don't have enough words to describe how thankful I am to God for sending me my perfect mate. Helpmeet. Absolutely beautiful Empress. Proverbs 31 woman. *My Dolcezza.* I've waited for this moment since I was a little boy observing my parents and their love for one another. There is no other woman on this planet that makes me feel the way you do. You mess with all my emotions girl. But baby, I love so you much. It would be an honor if you Tahira Inielle Aiyoki Zagori, would join me in a lifelong journey of love fulfilling purpose. Will you marry me?"

"Yes I'll marry you Tavario. Yes times infinity. I love you," Tahira cries hysterically.

"Do you remember these?"

"The Aquafire stone and silver ring; I gave them to my dad. How'd you get it?"

"When I went to visit your parents to ask for their blessing your father showed me some of your prized possessions, like your trophies and awards. Then I saw them in a tray decorated with sparkles. He told me that it was a tray you created when you were 4 years old at your first Vacation Bible School. He decided to put them there because you said it was **special**. I explained to him that I gave them to you. He said '*then you're the rightful owner.*' I had them ever since and asked a jeweler in Lux Point Milano to combine them and he designed it for me to give to you. This ring is a reminder of our journey and seeing it on your finger makes me smile. I love you," Tavario confesses, before embracing her.

BEST KISS EVER!! Kissing my dream man. Hehe. This is really happening.

Moments later the theatre was filled with all their loved ones. Everyone smiling, clapping, congratulating, and hugging them both. Official toasting was in order and the guests raised their glasses.

"To Tahira and Tavario," the audience cheers.

Tevaia walks over to Tahira, "See girl, I told you that he likes you."

"You did," Tahira giggles, "Now we're officially sisters."

Teviva joins them. "Welcome to the family Tahira. It's about time."

The three women hug.

Tavario glances at his sisters. "Can I interrupt this hug fest? I'd like to take pictures with my fiancée."

"Look at him. Thinks he's all grown now because he's getting married. You'll always be our little brother," Teviva coos, rubbing his hair. "Yes you will. Yes you will."

"Teviva, really?" Tavario replies, unamused at his sister's taunts.

"You two go ahead," Teviva laughs. "Now where's that husband of mine? Hashir…"

Music begins to play as they celebrate for the rest of the night.

25

On Friday night, Tahira and Tavario's families joined the church members for a prayer meeting. She'd been engaged for one day and hardly got any sleep.

"We're gathered here tonight for a special prayer meeting requested by the soon-to-be Mrs. Mikos," Pastor Hizaor informs the congregation. "I remember the day I dedicated this beautiful young woman standing before me. And I know that the entire church PRAYED, hmmmm, for this momentous occasion. Though we're months away from the wedding it is my honor as her Pastor to pronounce a prayer of blessing over this couple. Rebuking **every** guile of the devil against them, their family, and ministry. May they have a long and beautiful **spice** filled marriage. I don't want to go preaching a wedding day sermon now. Let's surround this couple. Honey, the oil please?"

Ankara hands her husband the anointing oil and joins him as they prayed for Tahira and Tavario.

Every word that came out of the Pastor's mouth made Tahira cry. To think that in a few months she'd marry the man of her dreams now turned reality. All that she'd been through had brought them to this place, surrounded by their family and loved ones. Tavario was truly God sent and she was glad that she never stopped believing in the impossible. She opened an eye and watched as he reached out to God on their behalf. Yes, this man was THE definition of a *Priest. Leader. Her Emperor. FINE like that.* As the prayer continued she couldn't help but blush. This was her husband.

Kaiora planned a surprise pre-bachelorette party for Tahira. The party started after the special prayer meeting and finished at 2AM; Kaiora decided to spend the night at the Zagori' household, for old times sake.

"Tahira, you have a phone call," Kaiora announces yawning.

"Who is it?"

"Your friend in Greece."

Tahira takes the phone. "Olympia, how are you?"

"I hear that official congratulations are in order," Olympia exclaims happily.

"Wow, how'd you find out so soon?"

"Your fiancé invited me to come for the proposal and engagement party, but I told him we have an assignment to complete."

"More Agaitimo sightings?" Tahira whispers.

"No," Olympia assures. "Even if there was, that's not for you to worry about."

"You have to send me your measurements. I need to order your bridesmaid dress."

"Already gave the information to Tavario."

"Will you be bringing a plus one?"

"As a matter of fact, yes."

"Xylon?" Tahira speculates.

"How'd you figure?"

"I saw the way he looked at you when you came on stage at **DECIMATION**.

Thankfully, we had no feelings for one another or I'd be jealous. He's a great man. Anyone willing to go through all of that just to protect someone they don't know gets points in my book. You're blushing. I'm happy for you, even though I know that Vassos was the love of your life."

"He'll always have a place in my heart," Olympia replies sadly.

"Are you moving to Starr Islands?"

"Actually, Xylon's moving to Greece. He's going to become a member of the NIU. When are you coming here?"

"Soon I hope. Will have to discuss it with Tavario."

"See you girl. Official countdown to your wedding. Can't wait for the BACHELORETTE PARTY!!" she shouts.

"Do you have to go back to St. Jannaio? We have a wedding to plan," Tahiti groans at sunrise.

"Mom, I trust your planning skills. I've already given the wedding coordinator all the ideas for the wedding. It'll be fine. If anything you can video call either me or Tavario. You have free reign. You two will work well."

"I really wish you could stay. The next time I see you will be a few days before you marry and leave me again."

"This is what you wanted for years. Don't get soft on me now."

"I won't, I won't. Lord please let these few months pass quickly so my baby girl can get married," her mother prays.

26

Tahira's 28th Birthday

Today was her 28th Birthday; 7 years after her 21st birthday. The number 7 signifying completion. Twenty years after the first time she saw Tavario on TV. Nothing was going to ruin this day. She tried to hold back tears, but cried remembering the disaster of her first nuptial. Then the crazy idea of agreeing to marry a man she didn't love. She would've definitely missed out on her blessing, God's best for her.

Early in the morning the Church mothers came to her bridal suite for one final prayer of blessings. The anointing oil poured from head to toe.

"My daughter today is the day that your father and I have waited for. Seeing you walk down the aisle to your husband. Though I'm sad that my only child will be whisked away to some foreign country, I'm thankful to gain the son I always wanted. Tavario is a wonderful man and I know he will love and cherish you like your father has done for me. Every love story is different and this one is for the movies. I promised I won't cry, but here I am. Happy 28th Birthday Tahira. Momma loves you baby girl."

"Awwww mom. You're the best. I love you."

"Happy Birthday to you, Happy Birthday to you, Happy Birthday Tahira Zagori soon to be Mikos, Happyyyyyyyy Birthdayyyyyyyy to youuuuuuuuu. And many more," Kaiora sings bringing in the cake.

"You don't want me to fit into my dress?"

"You don't have to eat any. I can eat your share. It's no problem."

"Girl, you know I want my birthday cake. Is it white chocolate?"

"You know it."

"Maid of Honor, can I see my bridesmaids now?" Tahira glances around the room.

"Here we are." Olympia and Siren enter the room modeling their dresses.

"We brought Greece to you. Here's something old."

"What is it?"

"Vassos' first Medal of Honor," Olympia hands her the medal.

"I can't take this," Tahira declines.

"He'd want you to have it."

"Thanks."

Siren places a heavy silver object in Tahira's hand, "Here's something borrowed."

"Your NIU pen?"

"For you to sign all your wedding day documents. Be very careful as it is an agent weapon," Siren warns.

Tahira stares at Siren apprehensively. "Oh my. Are you sure you don't want to hold on to it?"

"You'll be fine. I turned off the danger feature," she giggles.

Nizelli bounds into the bridal suite singing, "Special delivery. Special delivery. To aunty Tahira from uncle Tavario. Happy Birthday. He said don't open it until after the reception."

Kaiora pats Nizelli's head, "Good job son."

Tahira smiles at her nephew. "Thank you Nizelli. Where's your sister?"

"With daddy. She's crying a lot," he turns to Kaiora. "Mommy I think she's hungry."

"I'll be right out. Give me a minute girl?" Kaiora pleads.

"You go right ahead, can't have my niece crying."

"Sorry we're late. Our brother had us running some last minute errands," Tevaia declares when they enter the room.

"It's okay. I'm glad the rest of my bridal party is here."

"Look at my daughter-in-law. Beautiful. My son chose well. Even though I knew he would," Avela beams, kissing Tahira's cheeks.

"Mrs. Mikos you're too kind."

"Let's take an *usie*." Teviva holds up the camera as the foursome smile.

"This is it my daughter," Ramiro declares at the entrance of the church. "You are so beautiful and I am happy to give you away to Tavario."

"Thanks daddy for not giving up on me and setting me straight; even though I gave you a lot of resistance."

"One day you'll have children of your own and understand exactly what I went through. I'm glad that phase is over. You're about to be a **wife**." He kisses her cheeks. "Are you ready?"

"I am," she beams.

"I, Tavario Eaurelius Mikos, take thee, Tahira, to be my wedded wife, to have and to hold, from this day forward, for better, for worse, for richer, for poorer, in sickness and in health, to love and to cherish, till death do us part, according to God's holy ordinance; and thereto I pledge myself to you. I promise to always treat you like the Empress that you are."

"I, Tahira Inielle Aiyoki Zagori, take thee, Tavario, to be my wedded husband, to have and to hold, from this day forward, for better, for worse, for richer, for poorer, in sickness and in health, to love and to cherish, till death do us part, according to God's holy ordinance; and thereto I pledge myself to you. And I promise mmmm hmmm mmmm to *always* view you as the FINENESS that you are."

"Tahira and Tavario, by their solemn promises, freely made before God and in the presence of this assembly, have joined themselves to one another for love and for life. Those whom God has joined together, let no one put asunder. By the authority vested in me by the Holy Spirit and Country of Fortazonio, I now pronounce you husband and wife. Tavario you may now kiss your bride," Pastor Hizaor announces proudly.

The audience erupts in cheers and whistles as the newlyweds kiss. A kiss even the movies couldn't handle.

"You can open your present now," Tavario inclines to his new bride.

"Oh, I forgot all about it." Tahira tears open the package and cries. "Tavario, this is the BEST present ever. Thank you my husband."

"You like it?"

"LOVE."

"Greece, here we come."

"It's about time," Tahira giggles.

"I love you Mrs. Mikos," he kisses her.

"I love you too Mr. Mikos," she blushes.

The road that led to love was tumultuous, but as she looks at her husband resting on the plane in all his fineness, Tahira smiles, knowing that it was all worth it...

www.ingramcontent.com/pod-product-compliance
Lightning Source LLC
Chambersburg PA
CBHW031945240626
47153CB00003B/865